THE
HAUNTED REALM

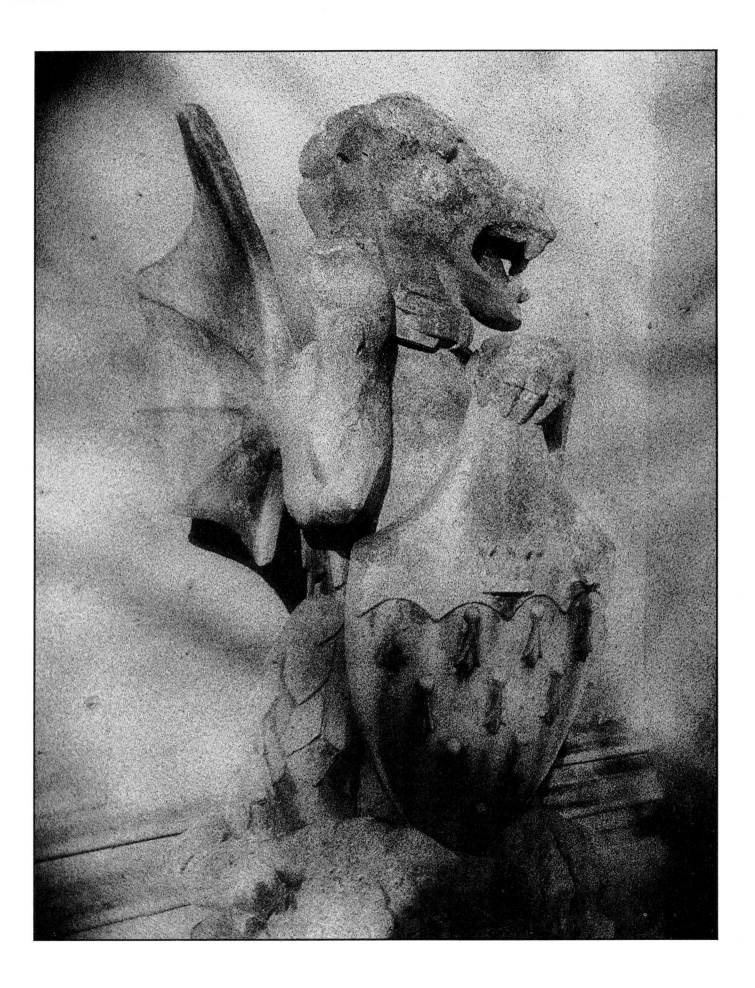

THE HAUNTED REALM

GHOSTS, SPIRITS AND THEIR UNCANNY ABODES

Photographs and Text by Simon Marsden

Introduction by Colin Wilson

E. P. DUTTON · NEW YORK

Frontispiece: Gargoyle, Knebworth House

Originally published in Great Britain in 1986
by Webb and Bower, Exeter, Devon,
in association with Michael Joseph Limited, London.

First published in the United States in 1987
by E. P. Dutton, a division of New American Library,
2 Park Avenue, New York, N.Y. 10016.

ISBN: 0-525-24498-0

USA

Designed by Vic Giolitto
Production by Nick Facer

Printed and bound in Italy by Arnoldo Mondadori Editore

1 3 5 7 9 10 8 6 4 2

First American Edition

CONTENTS

PREFACE

And travellers now, within that valley,
Through the red-litten windows see
Vast forms, that move fantastically
To a discordant melody,
While, like a ghastly rapid river,
Through the pale door
A hideous throng rush out forever
And laugh — but smile no more.

The Haunted Palace
Edgar Allan Poe (1809–1849)

I SUPPOSE it was natural that I should develop an interest in ghosts and all things supernatural from an early age as I spent my childhood in two archaic haunted houses. Both my father and elder brother were avid readers of ghost stories and I inherited the family's collection of books in the genre. My favourites were, and still are, Arthur Machen and M R James, mainly for their emphasis on mysteries as old as time itself, but also for the subtlety of their narrative.

Following on these days of playing hide and seek in ancient attics and wandering alone in deserted parklands, ever vigilant for the appearance of the 'family ghost', I was sent away to a monastic boarding school in the depths of the Yorkshire countryside. Here the pattern continued. Long and dark stone passageways were patrolled by cowled monks who asked one, at this impressionable age, to believe in all kinds of fantastic miracles or be condemned to wander as a 'lost soul' in the labyrinths of hell.

It was on my twenty-first birthday, when my father, a keen amateur photographer, gave me a camera, that I became instantly 'hooked' on photography. What intrigued me was the magic of time and light and the enigma of 'reality' that these elements conjured up. The first roll of film that I shot was of cardboard cut-outs of ghosts that I arranged in tableaux in the gardens.

My original aim in compiling this book was to select some unusual 'hauntings', some famous, some not so well known, and photograph them in such a way as to create a truly 'eerie' atmosphere. It was never my intention to try to prove the existence of ghosts, I simply wanted to inspire the reader not to take everything around him or her at face value; to show that what we are conditioned to believe is 'reality' may not be quite all it seems, if only we take the time to inquire.

I chose Britain and Ireland as 'The Haunted Realm' because they are the traditional home of ghosts, with so many historic houses and castles in remote settings, and because of the eccentricity of many of their inhabitants and the mythology of the ghost story that still persists. I did not include any 'modern day' hauntings, such as council houses or bingo halls, as mine is an unashamedly romantic approach to the genre and such places do not exist in my own particular 'fantasy world'.

I spent six months researching the book during the summer of 1974, compiling over 2000 suitable locations, although of course I learnt of many others from local people whom I met on my travels. During the next twelve years I must have visited almost 1500 of these locations. The strange thing was that throughout all the time that I was working on the project I felt I was being somehow guided and protected. It was as if everything had a predetermined pattern and the number of actual coincidences and synchronizations was uncanny.

As the work progressed I was greatly inspired and intrigued by the number of inexplicable stories of ghosts and other paranormal experiences that people recounted to me. I began to feel myself to be a catalyst, revealing a hidden reservoir of information that people were in the main too embarrassed to admit to anybody else for fear of being ridiculed. It is evident that this situation exists because we human beings appear to instinctively reject anything that we do not understand rather than face up to the unknown, tending only to believe in what suits us and what causes us the least anxiety.

To summarize my thoughts now that the book is complete would be to say that I feel mankind is far too quick to believe that science alone can cure all our ills and answer so many as yet unanswered questions. We appear to be either dismissing or forgetting much that our ancestors knew, our links with nature and the ancient magic from man's farthest and darkest past, things that are rooted indelibly within the mind of man. Science can explain anything away if one allows it to, just as all one's original thoughts and beliefs as a child can be eroded by the cynicism of one's elders.

NB As several of the houses included in this book are lived in and are not open to the public, the author asks that the reader respects their privacy.

INTRODUCTION

IN SEPTEMBER 1979, Simon Marsden, accompanied by a girlfriend went to visit the circle of prehistoric megaliths called the Rollright Stones in Oxfordshire, and afterwards went to look at the church in the village of Long Compton, two miles away. It is a beautiful church; but after only a few minutes, his girlfriend began to experience a curious sense of uneasiness. She decided to go and wait for him in the car. Marsden had one more thing he wanted to do before he rejoined her: the 'Close Field' next door to the church had an ancient mound that had been used for witchcraft ceremonies, and he wanted to photograph this. As he entered the field through a gate in the graveyard, the sky behind the mound looked stormy — the ideal background for a 'haunted' mound.

His camera was suspended round his neck on a strap. As he raised it to look through the view-finder, it was suddenly torn out of his hands by a force that seemed to deal him a violent blow — he describes it as feeling as if he had been hit by a thunderbolt. Shaken and frightened, he hurried back to the car. A few hours later, as he undressed in a hotel bedroom he discovered that his shoulder was covered with an enormous bruise. The odd thing was that it did not even hurt...

Like most true ghost stories, this one seems oddly inconclusive and unsatisfying. We like our tales of the supernatural to have some kind of climax — the secret room containing the skeleton of the murdered lover, the underground crypt where the wicked old baronet held his sinister orgies... The truth is that these tales are just as unsatisfying because most of them are pure invention, concocted to satisfy our craving for an explanation. Simon Marsden's story, on the other hand, has that flavour of authenticity that every 'ghost hunter' recognizes immediately. So before proceeding with this introduction let us see if we can begin to construct the outline of an explanation.

The Rollright Stones and Long Compton are in the centre of an area that has a long tradition of witchcraft. In 1875, a resident of Long Compton named John Hayward became convinced that he had been bewitched by an old lady called Ann Turner; he pinned her to the ground with a hayfork and slashed her throat and chest in the form of a cross with a billhook. Seventy years later, in 1945, an old labourer named Charles Walton was found nearby in exactly the same condition — pinned to the ground with a pitchfork, which had been driven through his throat; his throat and ribs had been slashed in the form of a cross with a billhook, which was still stuck in his ribs. In spite of all the efforts of Detective Superintendent Robert Fabian of Scotland Yard, the case remained unsolved. Local people simply refused to co-operate with the police. But one modern expert on witchcraft — Cecil Williamson — had more success. He learned that Walton was feared throughout the area as a 'witch'. He often sold charms, with a guarantee of a year's good luck — or freedom from catastrophe — and at the end of the year, was back at the door, demanding a further instalment to cover the next year. Few people had the courage to refuse. Walton also had a strange hobby — breeding large toads, and locals reported that he sometimes harnessed a toad to a toy plough and allowed it to run in a field. Now this is, in fact, a traditional piece of witchcraft to cause bad crops. And 1944, the year before Walton's murder, had been a year of exceptionally bad crops. The silence of the locals becomes understandable; they probably felt that whoever killed him had done them all a good turn.

Where is the logical connection between witchcraft and ancient stone circles? No one knows the precise purpose of megaliths like Stonehenge and the Rollright Stones, except that they were connected with some nature religion involving the sun and moon. But scientific investigation of the megaliths has uncovered some interesting fragments of information. When Professor John Taylor measured the force of a megalith near Crickhowell with a magnetometer, he discovered that its magnetism was far higher than that of the surrounding countryside, and that it appeared to take the form of a spiral around the stone. Since the mid-1970s, two ambitious projects, the Dragon project and the Gaia project, have been measuring the magnetic force and radioactivity of hundreds of megalithic sites. When my wife measured the radioactivity of two Cornish stone circles with a Geiger counter, she obtained some startlingly high readings. And I have described elsewhere* how, in 1975, I accompanied a 'dowser' to the stone circle called the Merry Maidens near Penzance and discovered, to my own astonishment, that I could also dowse. My friend showed me how to hold the forked rod — so it had a certain spring-like tension — and I walked towards one of the stones. I was intrigued when the rod immediately twisted upwards in my hands, and suspected that I had caused it myself by unconsciously 'twisting' the rod. But when the same thing had happened a dozen times, I had to admit that it seemed to happen without my volition, exactly as if I had carried a voltmeter close to a power line. Since then, investigation of many other sites — including the Rollright Stones — has convinced me that our ancestors chose these spots because they recognized an exceptionally high concentration of some earth force allied to magnetism. The force seems to fluctuate with the times of the year and the position of the sun and moon. The times chosen for the ceremonies — such as midsummer eve — were the times when the force was at its most powerful.

It can also produce unpredictable effects on the dowser. I found that about twenty minutes of dowsing at the Merry Maidens left me oddly exhausted. Good dowsers (and I do not include myself in this classification) may react so strongly to underground water that they have convulsions. In *Needles of Stone*, the dowser Tom Graves has described

* *Mysteries*, 1978, p117.

how, investigating the site of a megalith that had been destroyed, he encountered a force so powerful that it made him stagger backwards and sent a friend sprawling on the ground. Another site produced instant violent migraine.

Here, then, is a possible explanation of Simon Marsden's experience in the Long Compton field, with its prehistoric mound. But it is open to the obvious objection that he was not holding a dowsing rod at the time, but a camera. It sounds, in fact, altogether more like the traditional activities of the 'poltergeist', or 'banging ghost', which have been extensively recorded by students of psychical research. One such investigator, the late T C Lethbridge, has described how, on the island of Skellig Michael, off the coast of Kerry, he was examining the site of an ancient monastery when he was suddenly knocked flat on his face by a violent blow; when he sat up, the hillside was deserted. Lethbridge was a Cambridge don — and Keeper of Antiquities in the Museum of Archaeology — who discovered that his abilities as a dowser were an invaluable aid in archaeological research. About the force that knocked him down on Skellig Michael he writes (in *Ghost and Ghoul*, 1961): 'The happenings on the Skelligs, however, really come under the heading of poltergeist... A poltergeist is an invisible force, either without a mind behind it, or a mind so small that its actions appear to be completely irrational...'

It should be noted that Lethbridge calls the poltergeist a 'force', not a spirit. In fact, Lethbridge became convinced that there is a close connection between 'ghosts' — of the kind written about in this book — and the 'earth forces' involved in dowsing. He suspected, in fact, that so-called ghosts are a kind of 'tape recording'. This is a view first put forward in 1908 by Sir Oliver Lodge, who suggested that a haunting may be merely a 'ghostly representation of some long past tragedy', exactly like a gramophone record or an old piece of newsreel. According to the Lodge-Lethbridge theory — which is also held by Simon Marsden — violent emotions can be 'imprinted' on their surroundings (particularly, according to Lethbridge, when these surroundings are damp) — and later 'picked up' by people who happen to be 'sensitive' to them — like dowsers. Lethbridge had observed that some places simply have an unpleasant atmosphere, producing a sense of foreboding or gloom. He called these manifestations 'ghouls'. And a 'ghost', he thought, is a similar 'tape recording' that can be seen rather than felt. This seems to be confirmed by an observation contained in many reports of hauntings in the annals of the Society for Psychical Research: that in cases where a house has been rebuilt, a 'ghost' may be seen walking several feet above the floor or — in cases where the floor level has been raised by the builders — cut off at the knees.

Here, then, we have a basically rational and scientific theory that would explain the majority of hauntings described in this book. According to this theory, the 'tape recording' of strong emotions is more likely to happen in a place where the 'earth force' is strong rather than a place where it is weak. In 1977 I presented a typical case of this type on BBC television. In 1952, a couple named McEwan moved into Ardachie Lodge, near Loch Ness, and hired a

couple named McDonald to act as housekeepers. On the night of their arrival, the McDonalds were kept awake by footsteps in the corridor; then Mrs McDonald was petrified to see an old woman beckoning to her. Later, she saw the same old woman crawling along the corridor with a candle in her hand. Investigations revealed that the previous owner of the house had been an arthritic old lady named Brewin, who became so crippled that she had to crawl about on all fours. She suspected the servants of stealing from her and so used to crawl around at night holding a candle. Both families left the house, and it was finally bulldozed to the ground by the army in 1968.

When I presented the case, I had just come upon the works of Lethbridge, with his 'tape recording' theory, and also upon the odd fraternity known as 'ley hunters', who believe that the 'earth force' can be traced across the landscape in lines which are known as 'leys'. Sacred sites — like Stonehenge and the Merry Maidens — are often found on the crossing point of two or more leys, and — according to ley hunters — such places are more likely than most to be the sites of 'supernatural' occurrences. And it was a ley hunter named Stephen Jenkins, a retired schoolmaster, who wrote to me to say he had seen the programme, and had taken the trouble to get an ordnance survey map of the area around Loch Ness. It revealed, he said, that Ardachie House was the crossing point of no less than four major leys. I studied his evidence and had to agree that it looked highly plausible.

The tape-recording theory certainly seems to 'explain' about 90% of the cases in the present book (that is to say, the cases we can accept as authentic, and not as mere folklore or gossip), and when I first wrote about it — in *Mysteries* — I was convinced that I had found a logical explanation for most of the hauntings accepted as genuine by the Society for Psychical Research. Yet I had to admit that, in the case of the poltergeist, it still left certain problems unexplained. For how could a 'tape recording' knock Lethbridge on his face on a deserted island — or, for that matter, tear a camera out of Simon Marsden's hands? And here, a recent piece of scientific discovery came to my aid. In the early 1960s, the brain researcher Roger Sperry made the startling discovery that we have two people living inside our heads: the person you call 'you', and a total stranger. The brain has two halves — or hemispheres — so that when looked at from above, it looks rather like a walnut. The halves are joined by a bridge of nerves called the *corpus callosum*. Physiologists discovered that epileptic attacks can be prevented by severing the *corpus callosum*, which prevents the 'electrical storm' from passing from one side of the brain to another. It was Sperry who discovered that these 'split brain patients' had turned into two people. If a split brain patient was shown an orange with his left eye (which, for some reason, is connected to the right side of the brain) and an apple with his right eye (connected to the left side) then asked: 'What have you just seen?', he would reply: 'An apple.' Asked to write with his left hand what he had just seen, he would write 'Orange.' Asked what he had just written, he would reply: 'Apple.' When one split brain patient was shown an indecent picture with the right side of the brain, she blushed; asked why she was blushing, she replied: 'I don't know.' This demonstrates clearly that the person you call 'I' lives in the left hemisphere of the brain. The person who lives in the right hemisphere is a stranger.*

Now it had been known since the late nineteenth century that most cases of 'poltergeist haunting' tend to take place in houses where there is a teenager on the point of adolescence, or a disturbed child. Such a person is known to researchers as the 'focus' of the disturbance. (In a few rare cases, an adult may be the focus.) It seemed to me that Sperry's observation about the 'two selves' could provide a sound scientific explanation for the poltergeist: it is simply the person living in the right side of the brain. But how can that stranger cause objects to fly around the room? Here, it seemed to me, the answer could lie in those tremendous 'earth forces' that seem to be involved in dowsing. Dowsing is almost certainly a 'right brain' activity. The 'earth energies' (or the electrical field of underground water) communicate themselves to the right cerebral hemisphere, which in turn causes the contraction of the muscles that 'twists' the rod. In certain places — crossing points of ley lines, for example — these forces may be so powerful that they can send a dowser into convulsions. Lethbridge was undoubtedly a very good dowser; so perhaps the force that

* For reasons of compression I have been forced to crudely oversimplify this account, but it is basically accurate.

knocked him down was simply the same kind of earth force that almost sent Tom Graves sprawling?

Regrettably, I have been forced to abandon this theory — regrettably because I believe it is at least partially true, and it has the satisfying neatness and symmetry that characterize a good scientific hypothesis. But when, in 1980, I began to research a book on the poltergeist, I finally had to admit that there is a far simpler and more convincing explanation: that the poltergeist is a 'spirit'. I reached this conclusion with agonising reluctance, for I realized that, scientifically speaking, it placed me beyond the pale. I would far rather believe that poltergeists are manifestations of the right brain. The fact remains that the study of hundreds of cases of poltergeist activity, from medieval Germany to modern Brazil, left me in no doubt whatever that the poltergeist is some kind of spirit. I found myself so dismayed and irritated by this conclusion that I still insisted that it had no logical connection with a belief in life after death, about which I continued to be sceptical. Then, in 1984, I was asked to write a book on the evidence for life after death. Once again, I embarked on a lengthy study of the scientific evidence. And, once again, I ended by being overwhelmed by its sheer consistency. If the belief in spirits and life after death was basically a matter of superstition or wishful thinking, you would expect accounts to differ widely in their basic details. In fact, once a researcher has become familiar with a certain basic pattern, he can detect instantly when an account is genuine and when it is largely invention.

BROMPTON CEMETERY, LONDON

My own acceptance of the evidence for spirits and life after death has not turned me into an ardent spiritualist; in fact, I am rather inclined to avoid the subject. Yet I have to admit that, as an objective investigator, I find the evidence overwhelming, and I believe that anyone who takes the trouble to study it with an open mind will reach the same conclusion.

This does not mean, of course, that I reject the tape-recording theory, or the connection between 'hauntings' and earth forces. I believe that Lethbridge was correct to believe that the 'force' in certain places is exceptionally powerful, and that these places were chosen by our ancestors as sacred sites. (In the Middle Ages the Church issued a directive that, where possible, new Christian churches should be built on ancient pagan sites — apparently a recognition that these sites were somehow 'sacred' in themselves.) I also believe that these places were sacred because they could 'record' human emotions and feelings, so that centuries of worship could 'accumulate' an atmosphere that was conducive to religious exercise. This also means that they can 'record' negative feelings — disasters and tragedies — which can in turn produce unpleasant effects on those who are sensitive to them. Today's newspaper provides a case in point.* Deborah Pickering, formerly a staff writer on the *Financial Times*, described in court how she and her lover John Curry took over a pub called the Spectre Inn, in the village of Pluckley, Kent. She is reported as saying: 'Immediately I arrived I knew the village was evil: you can feel evil vibrations there... From the first moment I had the feeling we should not be there...' Pluckley, according to the *Guinness Book of Records*, has more ghosts than anywhere else in England. Mrs Pickering reports that her cat and dog would never follow her upstairs. 'Directly they got to the stairs, their hair would stand on end. I also felt there was a presence in the inn.' She and her lover began constantly quarrelling, until she finally fled. I have no knowledge of the topography of Pluckley, but would be prepared to wager that an ordnance survey map would reveal a record number of ley lines.

All this enables me to offer a tentative explanation of Simon Marsden's experience at Long Compton. Here, it seems, we have an area where certain natural forces (and I must emphasize that we may be dealing with nothing more 'occult' than ordinary earth magnetism or radioactivity) can produce some peculiar effects: they can 'record' human emotions and they can 'interact' with the human mind. Tom Graves describes how he arrived one midsummer morning at the Rollright Stones to find the smouldering ashes of a bonfire and the mutilated remains of a puppy — evidence that some witchcraft ceremony had taken place there on the previous night. He writes: 'The "atmosphere" in and around the circle could aptly be described as hellish; and even though the owner had an exorcism service held there within a couple of days, an unpleasant "buzz" — that's the only way I can describe it — could still be felt around the centre of the circle for nearly two years.' According to the Lodge-Lethbridge theory, this 'buzz' was basically a 'recording'.

The church at Long Compton and its adjoining field have also probably been used for similar ceremonies at some time. So the unpleasant sensation that drove Simon Marsden's girlfriend out of the church was probably another 'recording' — Graves's 'buzz'. But the force that tore Simon Marsden's camera out of his hand was almost certainly a poltergeist manifestation, expressing its displeasure at his intention of taking photographs.

It now seems to be a fairly well-established fact that poltergeists need to 'draw' their energy from some human source. The source, in this case — I would suggest — was Simon Marsden himself. If this theory is correct, then the 'bruise' on his shoulder was not a bruise, but a mark left by the withdrawal of energy, rather like the mark left by a leech.

I suspect that Simon Marsden himself would not feel particularly comfortable with this view. When I asked him about his own theory of the nature of ghosts, he said that he agreed with Lethbridge that they are basically 'tape recordings'. When I suggested that his experience at Long Compton revealed that he himself is 'psychic', he said that other people had told him so, but that the idea made him feel nervous — he added that he would prefer not to get too deeply involved in 'that kind of thing'. This is probably an attitude he shares with most people, including myself. When I began to research the subject in the late 1960s — for a book called *The Occult* — I quickly became convinced that our primitive ancestors were far more 'psychic' than we are, and that we have quite deliberately got rid of such powers, since they would be of no particular use to us in our highly mechanized civilization. But it also became clear to me that most of us possess the remnants of these powers, and that we could reactivate them if we wanted to. As soon as I began to write *The Occult*, I was startled by a series of odd coincidences. On one occasion, I decided to look up some particular topic, which I knew to be in one of the books on the shelf facing my desk. But I had no idea which one. Overruling my laziness, I forced myself to get up and take one of the books off the shelf. As I did so, I dislodged the volume next to it — which fell at my feet, open at the right page. This kind of thing happened so often that I finally came to take it for granted. I assume that when we require some particular piece of knowledge, we may be able to 'tune in' to it, using some unknown faculty, and that this produces the effect of coincidence.

When I asked Simon Marsden about his own experiences of such matters, he told me that he had also been struck by the number of coincidences that occurred when he started researching paranormal happenings. Again and again, he would fail to get the precise information he was looking for — and then stumble on it by accident when talking to a stranger or casually opening a book. One such experience was so striking that I suspect it comes under the heading of what Jung called 'synchronicity'. At the age of seven, Simon was given a pictorial encyclopedia of the world; it contained a rather frightening picture of an enormous tidal wave, about to break over a man and woman who were running along

* *Daily Mail*, 1 February, 1986.

the beach. For many years, he had a recurring nightmare of being on a beach when a tidal wave suddenly appeared. But in the mid-1970s, he went for a walk on the Yorkshire moors with his two sisters, and was fascinated by a deserted mine at Yarnbury, particularly by the eerie-looking building that had been the office. He climbed an old staircase, finding only empty rooms. Then, in the largest room, by a broken fireplace he found a copy of his old pictorial encyclopedia, lying open and face down; when he picked it up, he found that it was open at the picture of the tidal wave. 'It was a peculiar shock'; but from that time on, he ceased to have the nightmare.

For those who fail to see any logical connection between haunted houses and 'coincidence', it should be explained that the famous dictum 'As above, so below', attributed to the legendary founder of magic, Hermes Trismegistos, means: the pattern of the greater universe (macrocosm) is repeated in the smaller universe of the human soul (microcosm). It is self-evident that external events influence our states of mind (or soul); but perhaps the most fundamental tenet of 'occultism' is that the human soul can also influence external events — perhaps by some process of induction not unlike that employed in an induction coil. For the benefit of those whose knowledge of such matters is minimal, allow me to explain. If an electric current is passed through a coil of wire, it creates a 'field' around the wire. The strange thing is that if another coil is wound around the first one, with far more 'circles' of wire, a far more powerful current is somehow 'induced' in the second coil. So if you happen to be on the continent of Europe, where most electricity is a mere 120 volts, and you wish to use your British hairdryer, you merely have to buy a convenient little device in any electrical shop, and it will 'step up' your electricity from 120 to 240 volts. This extraordinary device is called, significantly enough, a transformer.

We can see that someone who knew nothing about electricity would regard it as preposterous that a mere coil of wire can double the strength of a current. They would want to know, to begin with, how the electricity could get from one coil to the other if they are not in direct contact. The answer is that the electrical vibrations in one coil communicate themselves to the other and induce a stronger current.

And, according to traditional 'occultism', the law 'As above, so below' means that the human soul can, under the right circumstances, induce its own 'vibrations' in the material world. One result of this process is 'coincidence'.

It should also be pointed out that a transformer can be used for the opposite purpose; if the current is passed through the coil with the most loops, a far weaker current will emerge from the other coil. And the problem with most human beings is that we use our soul-transformer the wrong way round. More often than not, a vague general sense of 'discouragement' or pessimism causes 'negative induction' in the environment. We are all familiar with that feeling that this is 'one of those days', and how, on such days, everything seems to go wrong. This, I would argue, is 'negative

induction', and it is basically due to our own negative attitudes. We also know those rare moods when everything seems to go right, and we have an odd feeling that they will continue to go right. This is positive induction. And one of the signs of positive induction is that curious coincidences keep on occurring.

Two paragraphs ago, I remarked that the human soul can induce its own vibrations *under the right circumstances*. If the 'ley hunters' are correct, these 'right circumstances' can be found in places where the 'earth force' is strongest; in that case, the 'induction' process works far more powerfully, for the earth force may be compared to a coil with many loops. But it also follows that such places can be used for negative purposes — hence black magic and witchcraft. And a person who happens to live in a house with a powerful 'field' may find it a mixed blessing. If he is inclined to negativity and pessimism, then he will increase the power of his own negative vibrations and cause himself a great deal of trouble. If his attitudes happen to be positive, then he can make use of the force for creative purposes...

I suspect that Simon Marsden's deep interest in the subject is another case of 'induction'. His grandfather owned a large fishing fleet in Grimsby, and this was passed on to Simon's father. The result was that Simon and his siblings spent their childhood living in a series of rather impressive houses, most of them with a reputation for being haunted. Between the ages of five and thirteen, Simon lived in Thorpe

Hall, near Louth, in Lincolnshire — a house that was so famous for its haunting that it was periodically opened to the public. The ghost of Thorpe Hall was a 'Green Lady', apparently a Spanish beauty who committed suicide for the love of the owner of the hall, Sir John Bolle. (There are various accounts of the tale in books of famous British ghosts.) Although Simon slept in the haunted bedroom (for some reason, he always seemed to find himself sleeping in the haunted bedroom in their various houses) he had no ghostly experiences. But his elder brother and sister claim to have seen the phantom coach of Thorpe Hall, and have apparently continued to insist on the truth of their story into adulthood, which Simon is inclined to accept as evidence that they are telling the truth.

In his preface, Simon writes of 'playing hide and seek in ancient attics and wandering alone in deserted parklands, ever vigilant for the appearance of the family ghost...' Then he was sent to a monastic boarding school in Yorkshire, where long and dark stone passageways were patrolled by cowled monks. At the age of twenty-one — after a period at the Sorbonne — he was presented with a camera by his father, and became deeply fascinated by photography, which he saw as an almost mystical affair. 'What intrigued me was the idea of being able to capture time at a thousandth of a second, the magic of light and the enigma of reality that these factors created.' The first film he took was of cardboard cut-outs of ghosts arranged in tableaux in the garden.

His apprenticeship was served as an assistant to two professional photographers, from whom he learned, among other things, how to produce a technically perfect print. But contact with other artists and writers, and experiences with the psychedelic drug LSD, made him feel increasingly frustrated with technical perfection; he began to feel that there was a barrier between himself and what he wanted to 'say'. And as he gradually learned to break down the barrier, and to put something of himself into his photographs, he began to experience the curious coincidences already mentioned, and began to feel that he was embarking on a journey into the unknown — into areas of deeper reality that are hidden from us by the superficial reality of the material world. And it was after a lengthy period in America that he decided to embark on the project of recording on film the most interesting haunted locations in the British Isles. In fact, his previous volume: *In Ruins, The Once Great Houses of Ireland*, is less concerned with haunted sites than with the poetry of ruins. But at the same time, he began accumulating the photographs of haunted houses that are gathered together in the present volume. In the course of twelve years, he has photographed about 1,200 old houses.

During this period he was struck by an observation that has occurred to everyone who has anything to do with investigating the 'paranormal', that we as 'human beings only believe what suits us. We reject what we don't understand, rather than face the possibility that there is still much in this world that we know nothing about'. He came to feel that his purpose was 'to inspire the reader not to take everything around him at face value — that what we are conditioned to accept as "reality" may not be quite all that it seems...'

He told me:

'We are losing our "sixth sense" in pursuit of purely material objectives. Our demand for uniformity and efficiency means that we allow ourselves no time to stop and enquire about what lies beneath the surface of everyday reality...'

A simple case in point is his photograph of Borley churchyard; he insists that the peculiar-looking object outlined against a patch of sky was not there when he looked through the view-finder. But he is speaking about far more than a few 'supernatural' oddities. His work is an attempt to capture a certain 'strangeness' in the external world, which can make us suddenly aware of the strangeness of the world inside ourselves. Simon Marsden is an explorer of the haunted realm of the human soul.

Colin Wilson

FEATHERSTONHAUGH CASTLE

Northumberland, England

THIS ancient and romantic castle of turrets, towers and ivy-clad walls lies in a wooded valley close to the banks of the South Tyne river. The oldest part of the castle dates back to the twelfth century but it has been greatly added to since then. The Featherstonhaughs were of very ancient lineage and featured prominently in the Border skirmishes against the Scots, but they finally lost their estates during the Civil War.

The castle will always be associated with the legend of the 'Ghostly Bridal Party'. The then Baron Featherstonhaugh, an extremely powerful and determined character, had arranged for his beautiful young daughter Abigail to marry a distant relative of his choice, but she had fallen in love with one of the sons of their traditional enemies, the Ridleys of Hardriding.

Lady Abigail reluctantly endured the wedding ceremony but was close to tears as afterwards the bridal party rode out for the traditional celebration hunt. The Baron and his wife stayed behind to organize the evening banquet. As evening began to draw in the Baron sat alone at the great table, goblet in hand, his face etched with worry. There was no sign of the returning party and he began to fear the worst. As midnight approached the torches began to dim and the embers in the fire to cool. The servants and minstrels sat in silence, not daring to move. The Baron then paced up and down the Great Hall with clenched fists while his wife hid her face in her hands.

Then suddenly the silence was broken by the sound of horses crossing the drawbridge. The great door slowly opened and in walked the bride and groom followed by the rest of the party. They made no sound as they moved through the furniture and the Baron gazed in horror, for all appeared drained of blood, and he realized that he was in the company of the dead. The servants shrank back in terror but as they did so a strong rushing wind swept through the hall and the spirits were gone. The Baron collapsed and from that day on was raving mad.

A search revealed the bodies of the hunting party in a nearby secluded glen known as Pinkyns Cleugh where they had been ambushed by the Ridleys who had intended to kidnap the bride. In the bloody battle that followed they had all been murdered. Lady Abigail had tried to come between her lover and her husband but had been accidentally slain. Both Ridley and her spouse had been killed in direct combat.

It is said that on the anniversary of this fateful day the phantom cavalcade can be seen winding its way towards the gates of this fairy-tale castle.

LOWTHER CASTLE
Westmoreland, England

THIS magnificent and spectacularly turreted ruin was once the home of the Lowthers, who became the Earls of Lonsdale. Abandoned in 1936 it is haunted by an eccentric member of this powerful family, Sir James Lowther, or 'Wicked Jimmy' as he was better known. He was described by Thomas de Quincey, author of *Confessions of an English Opium Eater*, as a 'True feudal chieftain in both appearance and deed, who took delight in expressing his disdain for modern refinement by the haughty carelessness of his magnificence.' He inherited the estate in 1784 and was greedy for power in both business and politics. A sinister figure, he was regarded with apprehension by his contemporaries and servants during his lifetime, and with absolute terror after it.

His downfall was his romantic nature and while he endured an unsuccessful 'arranged' marriage he fell in love with a beautiful young woman, the daughter of one of his tenant farmers. But as she was considered to be beneath his social standing he was forced to keep her as his mistress, albeit in great style at a manor house in Hampshire. For a while he was happy but when she grew ill and suddenly died he refused to accept that she was dead. His servants dared not mention it and he left her body lying on the bed as if nothing had happened; it is said that sometimes he would even dress her himself and sit her at the dinner table, until his servants were no longer able to endure the stench of her putrefying flesh.

He then had her moved back to another of his properties in Cumberland, to Maulds Maeburn Hall near

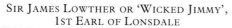

SIR JAMES LOWTHER OR 'WICKED JIMMY',
1ST EARL OF LONSDALE

Lowther, where her body was placed in a glass-lidded coffin which he left in a cupboard so that he could return to gaze at her. She was finally buried at Paddington Cemetery in London where he ordered a company of Cumberland militia to stand guard over her tomb for several weeks. Sir James then returned to Lowther where

he became subject to long fits of depression, walking alone in the woods for days on end. The estate began to suffer, the castle began to decay and wild horses roamed in the park. He died in 1802, unloved and unmourned.

It was said that at his funeral, his coffin swayed violently from side to side as it was lowered into the ground, and that his spirit returned to the castle where strange and turbulent noises were heard in the house and stables. It is said today that his spectral coach and ungroomed horses can still be seen being driven madly through the parklands of the castle on a moonlit night, whipped on by his manic and dishevelled ghost.

ATHELHAMPTON HALL

Dorset, England

She homed as she came, at the dip of eve
  On Athel Coomb,
Regaining the Hall she had sworn to leave...
  The house was soundless as a tomb
And she entered her chamber, there to grieve
  Lone, kneeling, in the gloom.

The Dame of Athelhall,
Thomas Hardy (1840–1928)

ATHELHAMPTON in Dorset was the inspiration for several poems by Thomas Hardy and the setting for his macabre short story 'The Waiting Supper'. The Martyn family lived at the Hall for almost three centuries. They were a Catholic family and there are several ghost stories dating from that period.

The most famous concerns a young lady of the family who kept a tame monkey as a pet. Sadly she had been jilted in love and decided to commit suicide. She fled through a secret door in the panelling of the Great Chamber, climbed the stairway to a room where she could be alone, shut the door and eventually killed herself. In her distress she had not noticed that the monkey had followed her through the panelling and by closing the last door behind her she had trapped the unfortunate creature on the stairway, where it starved to death. It is said that the monkey haunts the secret stairway and scratching noises have been heard against the panelling.

It is no surprise then that the family crest is a chained ape holding in its paw a mirror bearing its reflection, with the unnerving motto: 'He who looks at Martyn's ape, Martyn's ape shall look at him'. It is also said that until recently the main entrance gates to the Hall were surmounted by two stone apes which bore human faces, believed to be caricatures of politicians of the time. They have now sadly gone. The ape again appears in the magnificent Great Hall, portrayed in a stained glass window, this time with angels' wings.

The present owner, Sir Robert Cooke, has seen the ghost of a grey lady who has often been sighted in the Tudor Room. Once she was seen sitting in a chair by one of the housemaids who thought she was a visitor — the home is open to the public — and asked her to leave as it was getting late. At this point the lady got up and disappeared through the panelling. Other spectres include phantom duellists and a priest in a hooded black robe, who appear in the Great Chamber. There is also a ghostly cooper who hammers away at non-existent casks in the wine cellars.

During my visit the historical atmosphere of the house completely enveloped me and by the time I had walked out into the magnificent formal gardens with their impressive clipped yews, fishponds and fountains my thoughts were in another age. As I passed down the 'lime walk' in this trance-like state I suddenly looked up to be confronted by the stern, ghostly figure of Queen Victoria, a life size white marble statue. It took me several minutes to regain my composure and transport myself back to present times.

STATUE OF QUEEN VICTORIA, ATHELHAMPTON HALL

ELM VICARAGE
Elm, Cambridgeshire, England

THE outlandish events that took place in the 200-year-old rectory during the occupancy of Reverend and Mrs A R Bradshaw earlier this century are still debated in this beautiful and timeless Fenland village. According to Peter Underwood in his book *Gazetteer of British Ghosts*, the hauntings began with inexplicable footsteps in the house. Later the ghostly figure of a monk was seen. On one particular occasion Mrs Bradshaw claims she brushed past the ghost in a corridor and he told her, 'Do be careful.' She summoned the courage to ask his name and he replied, 'Ignatius the bell-ringer.'

Over the years Mrs Bradshaw met the ghostly monk many times and it appears that they became friends. She learnt that he had died over 700 years before in a monastery that had once stood on the site of the present vicarage. In those days the area had been low lying and there had been a constant threat of flooding from the Fens. It had been the duty of Brother Ignatius to act as a watchman and ring a warning bell when the level of the waters became dangerously high. One night he fell asleep and the waters began to rise. He awoke too late; several of the monks had already drowned in their cells. On his death his spirit was condemned to remain at the scene of his earthly disgrace. Mrs Bradshaw said that his ghost would appear at first as a faint outline and then materialize into the figure of a man of about thirty-three, dressed in an old, worn brown monk's habit and sandals. Ignatius appeared to the rector's wife many times and in several different rooms in the house.

Mr Underwood goes on to tell how, one autumn night, Mrs Bradshaw was sleeping in the visitors' room in the rectory as her husband was ill. Her dog, who usually slept in their bedroom, was behaving in a strange manner and refused to stay in the room at first. She was eventually able to drift off to sleep, only to be awakened by the sensation of something throttling her. She managed to switch on the bedside light and find that a tendril of wisteria growing on the outside wall had somehow made its way through the open window and wound itself around her neck. She tore it away, at the same time feeling herself being thrown across the bed.

Then a dark shape loomed over her and a pair of gnarled hands clutched at her throat. She thought she was about to faint as the hands tightened their grip but suddenly Brother Ignatius appeared and pulled them — or it — away. She fell back on to the bed exhausted, but again the spectre leaned over her and this time she could see its huge head and red face. Mrs Bradshaw managed to drag herself free and fled to her husband's bedroom. He later confirmed to investigators that her throat had been very badly bruised.

Mrs Bradshaw maintained that Ignatius later told her that the frightful spectre who had attacked her was the spirit of a man who had been murdered in that room years before. He added that by saving her life he had been released from his penance and his appearances would now become less frequent.

I was in Elm in June 1984 when I was told that the rectory had been empty for two years. The Reverend and Mrs Bradshaw are now both dead but the stories remain. An old lady who lives near the vicarage told me that she had known the Bradshaws well and that there had definitely been two ghosts there, one good, one bad. Before the bad one would materialize she said that the Bradshaw's dog would fly through the air. She asked me not to quote her name for fear of being ridiculed but swore that these facts were true.

Somewhat bewildered by these revelations I made my way through the graveyard towards the pub for a stiff drink. The stillness of the early evening and the dying light reflected on the skull and crossbones of several of the tombstones inspired my 'haunted' imagination. In the bar the landlord told me that the village was in fact 'wraithed' with ghosts. His wife's mother had seen the ghosts of a bride and groom in ancient dress walking by the church. The ghostly bride had indeed been seen many times. One night a motorcyclist collapsed through the front door of the pub after crashing because he had seen the girl's phantom standing by the church. I quickly accepted the landlord's offer of another drink.

GORMANSTON CASTLE

County Meath, Southern Ireland

GORMANSTON Castle in County Meath is the site of a strange and perhaps unique legend, even in this intangible and dream-like country.

In the hands of the Preston family, the Viscounts Gormanston, since 1363, the castle was then sold to the Franciscan Friars in the late 1940s, and is now known as Luke Wadding College. The coat-of-arms of the Gormanstons includes the figures of foxes and legend tells that whenever the death of a Viscount Gormanston is imminent scores of foxes leave their coverts and surround the castle, barking

GORMANSTON FAMILY COAT-OF-ARMS

and whining, only returning to their lairs after the Viscount's actual death.

The appearance of the foxes is chronicled in the records of the Preston family as far back as the seventeenth century. In 1860, when Jenico, the twelfth Viscount, was dying, foxes were seen about the house for some days. The foxes had come in pairs into the demesne and sat under the Viscount's bedroom window, barking and howling all night. The morning after his death they were found crouching in the grass in front of the house, but returned to their natural habitat after the funeral. What was so unusual was that they walked through the poultry and never touched them and they themselves were never attacked by the dogs, as if they were more than mere flesh and blood.

One of the sons of the fourteenth Viscount, who died in 1907, was keeping vigil over his father's body in the early hours of the morning in the family chapel when outside the door he heard whimpering and scratching noises. He opened the side door and saw several large foxes sitting there. He then went to the main door and, opening it, found two more foxes, so close he could have touched them.

The foxes' behaviour is said to date from the seventeenth century when a Viscount Gormanston saved the life of a vixen and her young, cornered on the Gormanston estate during a hunt. They first appeared when that Viscount was on his deathbed.

When I visited the castle it was the day before term began and I was met by one of the monks who showed me the coat-of-arms in the hallway. He told me that the locals still believed in the legend and that he himself had seen many foxes in the grounds.

[21]

SANDFORD ORCAS MANOR
Dorset, England

NEAR SHERBORNE, in a hollow almost entirely encircled by hills, lies the little village of Sandford Orcas. Next to the church is a driveway leading up to an impressive gatehouse; pass through and you are confronted by the sinister manor infamous for its legion of ghosts. High up on the gables the gargoyles, in the shape of crouching apes, leer down. The house is believed to have been cursed by a Saxon lord named Brithic who originally held the land, then known as Sandfordia. It appears that he was sent by his king as an ambassador to the court of Flanders where the count's daughter, Matilda, fell in love with him but he showed no interest in her. Matilda eventually became the wife of William the Conqueror of England but she never forgot the Saxon who rejected her and having confiscated all his land had him imprisoned for life.

In the twelfth century the manor was owned by Henry de Orescuilz and it is from a corruption of his name that Sandford Orcas derives. The present house was built by the Knoyles family in the fifteenth century and it is now owned by the Meddlycotts who, at the time I visited the house in 1975, rented it out to a Colonel Francis Claridge and his wife. The manor is magnificently furnished and contains many rare treasures, including a four poster bed of Spanish oak that bears the arms of Catherine of Aragon. I first caught sight of the Colonel in the gardens where he cut a particularly eccentric figure, a large portly man wearing khaki army shorts and sporting a monocle in one eye. He greeted me with a certain amount of suspicion but after a while agreed to take me on a tour of the house.

The tally of apparitions is almost endless and according to the Colonel it is impossible to retain any staff due to the awesome atmosphere. Many people have seen the ghost of a former tenant, a farmer who committed suicide by hanging himself from a pulley in the arch of the gatehouse. He usually appears in the gardens wearing an old-fashioned milking smock and Colonel Claridge even claims to have photographed him. Another spectre is that of an evil priest who has startled many guests in the middle of the night by standing over their beds holding a cloak out as if to smother them. It is believed that the house was once connected with Black Magic and that the priest had performed several Black Masses there. There are some very curious panels of stained glass set in a window over one of the stairways depicting satanic symbols which lend credence to this theory and now each bedroom has a crucifix hanging above the door.

The figure of a Moorish servant has been seen lurking in the damp corridors of the house. He is known to have strangled his master at Sandford Orcas but nobody knows why. But perhaps the most frightening story is that of a young man who was raised in the house and then sent to Dartmouth as a naval cadet at the age of fourteen. There he killed a boy and was sent back to Sandford Orcas having been judged insane. He was imprisoned in a room in the back wing of the house where he had to be restrained during the period from the new moon to the full moon and his screams still echo through the house on certain nights.

There are many other strange tales about the manor and the longer one stays there the more one begins to wonder whether the house itself and its occupants really exist or if they too belong to another time and another domain.

GUY'S CLIFFE

Warwickshire, England

ONCE described as 'The Mansion That Died', the house stands on cliffs above the bank of the River Avon near Warwick. Peering up through the trees from the river's edge, the outline of the ruined house, silhouetted against the sky, with its broken balconies, leaning chimneys and gaping windows, is a forbidding and melancholy sight.

The name Guy's Cliffe derives from the exploits of the Saxon hero Sir Guy of Warwick, whose eight-foot monument, now sadly vandalized, can still be seen in the ancient chapel. It is said that Sir Guy left his home and family for the Crusades where he performed many heroic deeds but, growing weary of warfare, he returned to England a changed man, both physically and mentally. Heavily disguised he took up residence in a hermit's cave below the house where he remained incognito, only revealing his true identity to his wife just before his death at the age of seventy. Shortly afterwards she hurled herself from the summit of the cliffs, drowning in the river below. The tall, bearded figure of Sir Guy's ghost has been reported near the house and cliffs.

The chapel is currently used as a Masonic Lodge, the mysterious environment providing a highly suitable setting. When I visited the chapel to see Sir Guy's monument I felt somewhat more intimidated by the atmosphere of the bizarre Freemasons' Temple than by his disfigured effigy, standing incongruous watch over their secret rites.

The old house itself is said to contain several 'cold spots' where visitors have felt that 'something awful' had happened. Apart from Sir Guy, another historical ghost has been seen near the house, that of Piers Gaveston, the favourite of Edward II, who was executed on nearby Blacklow Hill in 1312. His execution cavalcade wound its way from Warwick Castle past Guy's Cliffe and was seen at the beginning of this century by a group of women in broad daylight. They heard the sound of ghostly bells — his horse had been bedecked in finery and bells to mock his capricious nature — and the cruel taunts of his executioners.

Guy's Cliffe, with its caves, dungeons and apparitions, stands as a memorial to the past, but its eerie appearance makes it hard to believe that it will ever be anything other than 'alive' with ghosts.

WHITBY ABBEY

North Yorkshire, England

ARRIVING in the evening, as the sun was beginning to set, it was not difficult to imagine this fishing port on the Yorkshire coast as the inspiration for one of the world's greatest horror stories. It was in the summer of 1890 that Victorian writer Bram Stoker visited Whitby and from his diaries of that time we can see how impressed he was by the remoteness and romanticism of the town, by the huge mysterious ruin of the abbey in the strange evening light and most of all by the bats that circled the church tower. As a result of his brief three week holiday he envisaged the powerful and terrifying novel *Dracula*.

The town itself seems almost untouched by time, with its small Dickensian houses and narrow streets that wind their way up the hill towards the forbidding abbey, while in the harbour below, small old-fashioned fishing vessels float in on the incoming tide followed by wheeling armies of white seagulls. Whitby claims many ghosts of its own, not least that of the abbess, St Hilda, the daughter of the abbey's founder, who is often seen at night silhouetted against one of the windows of the abbey, dressed in a shroud. Another apparition is that of an ancient coach pulled by four headless horses which races along the clifftop near the abbey before it finally plunges over the cliff into the dark waters below.

But by far the most disturbing ghost is that of the pitiful Constance de Beverley in Walter Scott's *Marmion* who forswore her nun's vows for the brave but false knight, Marmion, whom she loved. For violating her vows Constance was condemned to be bricked up alive in a dungeon in Whitby Abbey. She can sometimes be seen cowering and pleading on the winding stairway that leads from the dungeon out into the daylight.

By then it was almost completely dark and we began to descend the hill once again, passing the graveyard below the abbey wondering whether we would sleep at all that night.

The Hermit's Chapel

Roche Rock, Cornwall, England

TRADITION tells of a dark spirit that wanders the loneliest parts of Bodmin Moor and whose despairing cries are still heard above the autumn gales. The spectre is believed to be that of Jan Tregeagle who was doomed to eternal torment for the sins that he committed during his lifetime. Tregeagle had been a stern and unpopular magistrate during the seventeenth century, using his position to amass considerable wealth. Part of this was paid in bribes to the clergy so that, despite his evil ways, he could be eventually buried in the consecrated ground of St Breock's churchyard, but this precaution was of little avail for within a few years he was to be summoned from the grave.

A dispute had arisen between two local families over the ownership of some land near Bodmin and Tregeagle, while alive, had acted as lawyer to one of the claimants. By committing fraud, Tregeagle had made it appear that he himself held the deeds to the land in question. At the Assize Court after Tregeagle's death, just as the judge was about to begin his summing up, the defendant pleaded to be able to call one further witness.

The atmosphere in the courtroom grew ominously cold and the defendant appeared to have gone into a trance. Suddenly, to the astonishment of the assembly, Tregeagle's ghost materialized in the witness box. Standing before the judge the spirit revealed that the accused had been a victim of his fraud, and the jury gave their verdict in the unfortunate man's favour, at the same time summoning the local clergy who felt it their duty to save Tregeagle's soul. They decided to set him a task that would engage him for all eternity; so long as he toiled at it he would be saved from the Evil One. Bound by spells he was given a cracked limpet shell and instructed to empty the mysterious Dozmary Pool, a bottomless lake on Bodmin Moor. He was guarded by a pack of headless hounds who waited to carry him off if he should ever cease his labours.

One night, greatly disturbed by the ferocity of a storm, Tregeagle's spirit defied the demons and fled across the moor, the evil pack in hot pursuit. They had almost caught up with him when he reached the chapel at Roche Rock and, thrusting his head through the east window, he attempted to gain the sanctuary of the church, but while his head remained within the chapel, his body remained outside, exposed to the fury of the storm and the snarling fangs of the hounds of hell. His screams could be heard for miles around. After a while the priest of the Rock could stand it no longer and, calling on the help of the Almighty, he led Tregeagle down from the Rock and banished him on to the moor.

And so to this day, the ghost of Jan Tregeagle must wander abroad performing endless futile tasks, an assignment he inherited by selling his soul to the Devil.

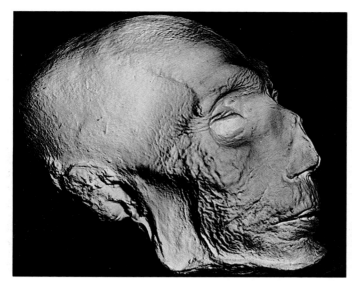

THE EARL OF BOTHWELL'S MUMMIFIED HEAD

HERMITAGE CASTLE
Roxburghshire, Scotland

ARGUABLY one of Scotland's most notorious castles, this massive border fortress dating from the thirteenth century has a particularly savage and cruel history. The haunted castle repeatedly changed hands between England and Scotland over the centuries and each time usually meant a gruesome end for its previous owner. It was held at different times by the great families of Dacre, Douglas and Bothwell. Among Hermitage's troubled ghosts is that of Alexander Ramsay, Sheriff of Teviotdale, who was thrown into one of the castle's dungeons and left to starve to death by the then owner Sir William Douglas. Another ghostly visitor is Mary Queen of Scots who, in great distress, rode from Jedburgh to Hermitage and back over the wild moors in a single day, a distance of over fifty miles, to comfort her lover the Earl of Bothwell when he lay wounded at the castle. She caught a fever from this brave act from which she almost died. Bothwell's phantom has also been seen here.

The most malevolent ghost of Hermitage is that of Lord de Soulis, the infamous practitioner of the Black Arts and a vicious child murderer. His spirit still haunts the castle and its surrounds, searching for young children to kidnap as he had done when alive. He would imprison them in the castle's dungeons and then murder them in order to use their blood in his foul magic rituals to summon up his 'familiar', known as 'Robin Redcap', an horrific vampire-like figure with long fangs.

Rumours eventually led the local people to realize what was happening to their missing children. In the dead of night they stormed the castle and took de Soulis prisoner, then threw him into a cauldron of boiling lead.

During my visit I felt the grim, solitary and eerie building to be deeply forbidding, and I found it easy to believe why the novelist Sir Walter Scott had commented that the castle was supposed to have partly sunk beneath the ground, no longer able to support the load of iniquity which had long accumulated within its walls. I was glad to leave.

[29]

MORETON CORBET CASTLE
Shropshire, England

THIS beautiful and melancholy Tudor ruin is both cursed and haunted. It belonged to the Corbet family, who include a corbeau or raven in their coat-of-arms. The house was begun in 1606 by Sir Robert Corbet, who is said to have brought the plans for the design of the mansion from Italy, but he unfortunately died of the plague before the building had progressed very far. His successor, Sir Vincent Corbet, continued the work. During these times King James I was persecuting the Puritans and, although Sir Vincent was not himself a Puritan, he did not wish to see them treated so harshly. One of their number, a neighbour called Paul Homeyard, was a friend of Sir Vincent and he gave the neighbour refuge in his home. But as the Puritans' aims became more fanatical and militant he was forced to tell Homeyard that he was no longer able to hide him from his pursuers. Homeyard fled into the surrounding countryside where he hid in caves and ate wild animals and berries until he felt he could safely flee from the area.

One day the thin and haggard figure of the Puritan passed near the castle, where he saw Sir Vincent surveying the progress of the building work. He approached Sir Vincent and in a vindictive, cracked voice is said to have uttered the following curse:

> Woe unto thee, hard-hearted man, the Lord has hardened thy heart as he hardened the heart of Pharaoh, to thine own destruction. Rejoice not in thy riches, not in the monuments of thy pride, for neither thou, nor thy children, nor thy children's children, shall inhabit these halls. They shall be given up to desolation; snakes, vipers and unclean beasts shall make it their refuge, and thy home shall be full of doleful creatures.

The prophecy was fulfilled and the mansion never finished. The roofless remains still command the countryside and on a moonlit night the ghost of the frail and fleeting figure of the unhappy Puritan can still sometimes be seen wandering through the desolate halls.

MONUMENT TO THE CORBET FAMILY,
MORETON CORBET CHURCH

BARCALDINE CASTLE
Argyllshire, Scotland

BUILT by the Campbells in the sixteenth century, the castle lies close to Loch Creran and it was here that the opening scene of an uncanny supernatural drama was acted out. In the eighteenth century the Laird of Barcaldine was Donald Campbell, who was tragically murdered in the grounds of the castle by a Stewart of Appin, sworn enemies of the Campbells. His murderer, aware that he was in great danger of reprisal in Campbell territory, devised an ingenious escape that would put him above suspicion. He would ride to nearby Inverawe Castle, another Campbell stronghold, before the news reached there and ask for hospitality which Duncan Campbell, the murdered man's brother, could not refuse by the unwritten 'Law of the Highlands'. He would surely be safe in such surroundings.

Suspecting nothing Duncan Campbell begrudgingly took him in and the two men wined and dined together in an uneasy alliance. Finally they retired to their different rooms and fell asleep. During the night Duncan was woken by strange sounds in his room. When he opened his eyes he saw the blood-spattered figure of his brother standing over him. Donald's ghost accused him of harbouring his murderer and pleaded with him to take revenge. Duncan, unable to discern whether he was dreaming or not, and bound by the sacred Highland Law, did nothing.

Three times the phantom appeared but Duncan would not be persuaded. On the last visitation the spirit glared at him with real hatred and uttered these words, 'Brother, I will not bother you again until we meet at Ticonderoga.' Unable to understand this prophecy Duncan could only lie awake thinking what he should do. As dawn approached he decided, against his code, to interrogate his unwelcome guest. Alas, it was too late, as the Stewart had already fled.

Some years later Duncan Campbell joined the Black Watch and in 1758 the regiment was sent to America. In July of that year he was killed in a battle with the French at a fort called Ticonderoga. Duncan's body was buried in America but his remorseful ghost returned to haunt Inverawe, and Donald Campbell's ghost has reputedly been seen at Barcaldine, where he still seeks revenge on his Stewart killer.

Newstead Abbey

Nottinghamshire, England

In the dome of my Sires as the clear moonbeam falls
Through Silence and Shade o'er its desolate walls,
It shines from afar like the glories of old;
It gilds, but it warms not — 'tis dazzling, but cold.

Newstead Abbey,
Byron (1788–1824)

THIS GOTHIC seat was originally a priory of Black Augustine Canons but in 1540 it was turned into a mansion by Sir John Byron and remained the ancestral home of the Byron family for almost 300 years. There is an ancient belief that those who alter or deface sacred buildings are plagued by ill-luck and it is certainly true to say that misfortune dogged the family during their years at Newstead. There are also several 'restless spirits' that are said to still wander the house and grounds. That the final Lord Byron to inherit the estate should have been the famous poet was in itself fitting as the romance of the Gothic architecture and the numerous lakes and follies perfectly complemented his own character. He loved Newstead dearly and wrote several poems on the abbey and its history.

When Byron inherited the property it was in a state of advanced decay. His predecessor, 'Devil Byron' as he was

LORD BYRON

known, was said by some to have been a madman. He deliberately ran down the house and grounds to ruin the inheritance for his son. He died alone in the servants' wing, by then the only habitable part of the house. The poet was

indeed a very handsome man, despite the handicap of a club-foot from birth. His eccentric behaviour and amorous adventures are well known, especially his affair with the beautiful and tempestuous Lady Caroline Lamb. One of Newstead's ghosts is Sophia Hyett, the daughter of a bookseller. She was infatuated with the poet and her spirit cannot rest without him.

The most famous of Newstead's apparitions is that of the

INTERIOR, NEWSTEAD ABBEY

'Black Friar'. The identity of this 'lost soul' is not known, but his appearance invariably foretold a crisis in the family. Byron himself claimed to have seen the phantom on the eve of his wedding to Annabella Milbanke. He later described his marriage as the most unhappy event in his life.

> By the marriage-bed of their lords, 'tis said,
> He flits on the bridal eve;
> And 'tis held as faith, to their bed of Death
> He comes — but not to grieve.
> *Don Juan*

Another spectre is that of the benign sixteenth-century figure of 'Little Sir John Byron, of the long beard' who for many years after his death was said to descend from his portrait in the library and be seen sitting beneath it peacefully reading a book.

Perhaps the most unusual ghost at Newstead is that of the poet's pet Newfoundland dog, Boatswain. Byron was broken hearted when the dog died and buried him on the site of the Black Canons' high altar. He asked to be buried there too when his time came, alongside probably the most constant friend he had in his tumultuous life, but his wish was not granted and perhaps this is why the phantom hound still wanders the grounds looking for his master.

> To mark a friend's remains these stones arise,
> I never knew but one, and here he lies.

> (the final lines of Byron's epitaph to Boatswain)

LONG MEG AND HER DAUGHTERS

Cumberland, England

THE Druidic stone circle known as 'Long Meg and her Daughters' lies in a beautiful and remote position high up on the edge of the Cumbrian Pennines. Legend tells that the exact number of stones can never be accurately counted; I totalled sixty-one the first time and sixty-six the second. The largest pillar is known as 'Long Meg' and is eighteen feet high, standing apart from the main circle.

This was, and still is, a very sacred site and nobody in the vicinity was surprised when, some time ago, a certain Colonel Lacy tried to remove the stones by blasting, he and his workmen were frightened away by the ferocity of a sudden storm.

How the circle came by its name is uncertain. Some say that Meg and her daughters were a coven of witches who were turned to stone for performing their infamous 'rites' here. Another version claims that the maidens of the nearby village, Little Salkeld, met with the same fate for dancing here on the Sabbath. Whatever the truth may be, as the evening sun began to set on the circle, and the shadow from Long Meg's stone lengthened, the feeling of ancient power and mysticism was overwhelming.

SPIRITS DANCING AROUND A STONE CIRCLE

Watton Priory

East Yorkshire, England

THE current tenants of Watton Priory are members of the 'Sealed Knot' an English Civil War Society, dedicated to recreating the life and warfare of the seventeenth century. They say that the priory itself is riddled with secret cupboards and passages and there is also a river running beneath the building. Although the house is chiefly built in the Tudor style it also incorporates the remains of an eighth-century nunnery, and a medieval priory. It has several ghosts but the two main spectres are both women and both of them are grieving over their lost children.

The first of these sad ladies was the owner of the house during the Civil War, and was a devoted Royalist. On hearing of the advance of Cromwell's troops in this neighbourhood and the rumours of their marauding deeds, she hid her silver and jewellery and then herself and her child in a secret room at the priory. Alas she was discovered and as she resolutely refused to reveal the whereabouts of her valuables they first grabbed the child and beat it to death against a wall and then decapitated her. The room where these infamous deeds took place is entered by a secret door in the panelling and it joins with a secret stairway down to the moat. The room is reputed to be haunted by the ghost of a headless lady in blood-splattered garments, holding an infant in her arms.

The second ghost is that of a nun who has been seen wandering the fields near the priory between the house and the nearby church. Her story is equally tragic. It is said that in the twelfth century Henry Murdoc, the Archbishop of York, placed a four-year-old girl in the nunnery at Watton to be educated as a nun. Her name was Elfrida. As the years passed she grew into a beautiful young woman and as her body began to portray her womanhood the other sisters, who were mainly middle-aged, or older, became jealous. Elfrida began to tire of the routine of the convent and became rebellious. She longed to see more of the outside world and to mix freely with men, as she felt her beauty deserved.

It so happened that the Gilbertine priory had been divided into a nunnery and a monastery and on infrequent occasions certain monks entered the nunnery for consultations with the prioress. Elfrida fell passionately in love with one of these monks. They began to meet at night via a secret passageway, but the other nuns quickly became suspicious.

The monk, fearful of the consequences should they be caught, abandoned the monastery for the secular life. This confirmed the suspicions of the nuns and Elfrida was summoned before the assembled sisterhood.

Unable to conceal her guilt from the prying eyes of her accusers Elfrida confessed. Astonished at such an open avowal the sisters, with zealous resentment against the poor woman, looked at each other, and at length clapped their hands and, like wild animals, rushed upon the unhappy girl, tore off her veil, and assaulted her even though she was pregnant.

They then debated what punishment they should inflict upon her. Some said she should be burnt alive, others flayed alive, and there were even some who wished her impaled upon a stake. The more bloodthirsty punishments were suggested by the younger nuns, but the elders were more restrained.

She was eventually stripped naked and stretched out on the floor in a dungeon where her wrists and ankles were manacled and she was whipped until her blood flowed. She was kept chained in the cell and fed only bread and water.

The nuns and monks then decided to trap her lover. A monk disguised himself as a woman and lay in wait in the secret passage that they still used, at the appointed time of the rendezvous. Her lover was caught and the nuns insisted that he be handed over to them for interrogation. They took him to an unfrequented part of the convent and committed brutal and unspeakable atrocities against him, all the time making the pregnant Elfrida watch. The same week a baby boy was born to Elfrida, which the nuns took from her, and shortly afterwards she died of her mistreatment and a broken heart.

Amongst other ghosts seen by the owners are a small man dressed in brown jacket and trousers in the garden and a Cavalier who leans against a non-existent mantelpiece in the bedroom. The owners say that the ghosts do not appear now as much as when they first moved in, and suggested that perhaps they were getting used to the new inhabitants.

The thought crossed my mind that perhaps the owners were so involved in living out their Civil War fantasies that the spirits would accept them quite readily in such an authentic Royalist environment.

BISHAM ABBEY

Berkshire, England

THE remorseful ghost of the brilliant but tyrannical scholar Dame Elizabeth Hoby appears at Bisham Abbey where she is seen washing her hands in a spectral basin that floats before her. It is said that she is trying to remove the bloodstains of her retarded son whom she continually flogged and finally imprisoned for his laziness and untidiness at his lessons.

The thirteenth-century abbey lies on the banks of the Thames in Berkshire and Dame Hoby's remarkable effigy can be seen in the chapel nearby. She died in 1609 a miserable and remorseful old lady, her youngest son William the cause of her guilt.

William's intellect had never lived up to her expectations and one day, when he had tried her patience to the limit and she had whipped him soundly with no effect, she decided to lock him in a dark room to teach him a stern lesson. That same day Lady Hoby received a summons from Elizabeth I, with whom she was on friendly terms, but before leaving she forgot to tell her servants of William's punishment and to give them instructions about when to release him. By the time she returned several days later he had tragically starved to death.

In the nineteenth century, when repairs were being carried out in the house, a number of heavily blotted exercise books, stained with tears and bearing the name William Hoby, were discovered hidden between the skirting board and the floorboards.

Lady Hoby's ghost has been seen in both the house and the gounds but the strange fact is that it appears in 'negative' form, wearing a white dress, but with black face and hands.

MONUMENT TO DAME ELIZABETH HOBY, BISHAM CHURCH

CASTLE BERNARD

County Cork, Southern Ireland

ASTLE Bernard's story is full of tragedy. The ghost of a Bernard child is said to haunt the top of one of the castle's many towers, from where he lost his footing and fell to his death through a trap-door, while trying to strike bats and swallows with his battledore.

On 21 June 1921, during the Irish Civil War, the then Earl and Countess of Bandon were caught off guard by the IRA during a dinner party. They and their guests were commanded to leave the house and were forced to watch from the lawn as the family's possessions and the house they loved were put to the torch. Lord Bandon was then kept a prisoner for three weeks, being moved from place to place in the dead of night in an old cart, the sides of which cut his flesh to the bone.

There are locals who say that the sad spectral scene of the fire is re-enacted at the now ruined castle on certain nights of the year, in what is just one more grim and nightmarish chapter in Ireland's troubled history.

Gothic window, Castle Bernard

WALLINGTON HALL
Northumberland, England

WALLINGTON in Northumberland was originally a medieval castle but in 1688 Sir William Blackett started to build the hall that now stands on this site. The haunting is of a particularly unusual and disturbing kind and one for which there is no apparent cause or explanation.

It is best recorded in the memoirs of the Victorian author Augustus Hare, written during a visit he made there in 1862. He appeared to have been immediately impressed by the strangeness of the house and wrote:

> There are endless suites of huge rooms only partly carpeted, with eighteenth-century furniture partly covered with faded tapestry. The last of these is the 'ghost room' and Wallington is still a haunted house: awful noises are heard through the night; footsteps rush up and down the untrodden passages; wings flap and beat against the window; bodiless people unpack and put away their things all night long and invisible beings are felt to breathe over you as you lie in bed.

Mr Hare found his bedroom 'quite horrid'. It opened into a long suite of desolate rooms through a door without a fastening and so he pushed a heavy dressing-table with its weighty mirror against it to keep out whatever might try to come in. He appears to have seen nothing but passed an uneasy night. Some people believe the ghost to be a headless lady but as there is no record of her having been seen, this theory cannot be verified.

Augustus Hare was equally struck by the eccentricities of the human inhabitants of the house. Although he remarked on his hospitality, his host, Sir Walter Trevelyan, was never known to laugh. He was 'a strange looking being with long hair and moustache and an odd, careless dress'. His conversation was so curious that Mr Hare made a point of following him around the house just to take notes of what he said.

Lady Trevelyan, a small woman with sparkling black eyes, was an artist and equally bizarre. She experienced what she called 'the most extraordinary feels' in the house. She rarely attended to her home and it remained in a state of almost continual chaos. There was another strange being in the house, a Mr Wooster, 'who came to arrange the collection of shells four years previously and had never gone away. He looked like a church-brass incarnated and turned his eyes when he spoke to you, till you saw nothing but the whites'.

The memory of these strange characters, the supernatural occurrences and the presence of four weird stone griffins' heads, retrieved from some demolished gates in the City of London by Sir Charles Philip Trevelyan in 1928, inspire the truly eerie atmosphere that I believe could not fail to impress the present day visitor.

LADY PAULINE TREVELYAN (1816–1866)

SIR WALTER TREVELYAN (1797–1879)

GRIFFINS' HEADS, WALLINGTON HALL

COLD ASHTON MANOR

Gloucestershire, England

IN the late 1930s, when Lady Winifred Pennoyer lived at Charterhouse, there occurred a strange and unusual haunting concerning the manor house at nearby Cold Ashton. She had invited her dear friend Olive Snell to stay for a few days. Olive was a portrait painter of repute and was keen to see her friend and show her some of her latest commissions. It had been a particularly ferocious winter and Lady Winifred advised her friend to set out early so that she would arrive in time for tea, as it was difficult to find one's way in the dark.

Olive was very much her own mistress and it was not until well after midday that she finally began her journey. Although bitterly cold the sun was shining and she was entranced by the landscape, driving at a leisurely speed to take in the breathtaking views of the countryside.

It was not long before the light began to fail and to her dismay, she found that she had wandered from the route that her friend had given her. After a few miles she came to a small village and ahead of her saw an extremely beautiful house, behind large wrought-iron gates with stone pineapples on either side. She got out of her car, opened the gate, and walked up to the front door. She rang the bell and as she stood waiting for somebody to answer, she noticed a powerful dank and musty odour. After a while an old man, who she presumed to be the butler, opened the door. She explained her predicament to him but as she spoke she saw an almost vacant gaze in his eyes as if he were looking straight through her. When she had finished, he smiled reassuringly, gave her instructions for finding her hostess's house, and in return she gave him half-a-crown.

Olive went back to her car and it was not long before she was turning into the driveway of her friend's home. By the warmth of the fire she related her story to Lady Winifred, who listened with surprise and finally suggested that they motor over there the next day, as she knew the house which answered to that description had been empty for many years. In the meantime she suggested that her friend should get a good night's sleep.

When they arrived at the house next day they found, much to Olive's surprise, that the gate was locked and the garden overgrown. They had to obtain the key from the gardener and having opened the gate with some difficulty, they approached the front door. There, lying on the step, was her half-crown.

ALLOA TOWER

Clackmannanshire, Scotland

THE hereditary curse upon the Erskines, Earls of Mar, has no equal in the annals of history as a prophecy of doom that was horrifyingly realized down to almost the last detail. That the title Earl of Mar is very ancient is not in doubt but there is some argument over who actually uttered the curse. Some say it was Thomas the Rhymer, the thirteenth-century Scottish Merlin, but it is more likely to have been the Abbot of Cambuskenneth whose abbey was sacked by the Earl of Mar in the sixteenth century.

What gives this particular prophecy its macabre authenticity is that it was well known by word of mouth and in print long before the predictions came to pass. 'The Curse of Alloa Tower' as it was usually called, is too lengthy to record in its entirety but the following précis includes the important omens:

> The family would become extinct and their lands would be given to strangers; an Erskine would see his house burnt where a king was raised and his wife would die in the fire; three of her issue would never see the light; horses would be stabled in the Great Hall and a weaver would throw his shuttle in the Chamber of State; but when an ash sapling should spring from the topmost stone of the tower then the curse would have run its course.

One hundred and fifty years later, after the battle of Sheriffmuir in 1715, the Erskines who had supported the defeated 'Old Pretender', had their titles forfeited and their lands were sold to the Earl of Fife; in 1801 John Frances Erskine watched as Alloa Tower, the childhood home of James VI, was accidentally burnt. His wife was killed in the fire; three of their numerous children had been born blind and remained so all their lives.

Early in the nineteenth century, during rumours of a French invasion, a troop of cavalry was stabled in the one-time Great Hall. Later, in 1810, some visitors to the Tower found a weaver, who had been evicted from a house in the town for rent arrears, established there and working in the Old Chamber of State. Finally, between 1815 and 1820, an ash sapling grew and flourished on top of the Tower.

And so, almost 300 years later, the prophecy had ended but too late to save the thirteenth-century Tower which still stands, incongruously surrounded by the modern town of Alloa, a grim reminder of the curse. It has remained empty for many years and the once grand porticoed doorway is now daubed with modern graffiti.

Over the doorway one can still find the Erskine coat-of-arms showing a hand grasping a dagger. Their motto reads 'Je Pense Plus'. The Tower is now the refuge of pigeons and rats.

MAIN ENTRANCE DOOR, ALLOA TOWER

COGGESHALL
Essex, England

IT is somewhat hard to imagine that this picturesque and sleepy little village in Essex should have the reputation of being one of the most haunted regions in England, but on a visit to my sister and her family, who have lived here for the last twelve years, I learnt that the number of alleged hauntings are numerous.

I was told that Cradle House, near Markshall Old Rectory, used to be the secret meeting place of the monks from Coggeshall Abbey and that a ghostly procession of white-clad figures has been seen floating through the grounds. Poltergeist activities have been recorded at 47 Church Street, where a secret room was discovered some years ago. The house used to be an Inn and people have felt a strange 'presence' there. At Guild House in Market End mysterious lights have been reported emanating from an attic room and visitors have reported seeing the phantom of a little old man staring at them from the foot of the bed in the middle of the night.

Coggeshall is set deep in the heart of East Anglian 'witch

WITCHES' SCENE, GOYA

country' and it is recorded that in Essex alone, between 1560 and 1680, over 550 people were accused of witchcraft. In fact the last witch to have been executed in England is widely believed to have been Widow Comon of Coggeshall, in 1699. According to the Reverend James Boys, the then

[50]

REFLECTION IN WINDOW, CHURCH STREET

Vicar of Coggeshall, she admitted that the Devil was her master and that she had liaised with him. She said that he had 'goggle' eyes and rough hands and she was later accused of suckling his imps with her own blood.

There are those who say that witchcraft is not dead and it occurred to me that to find an explanation for this 'troubled' area, with its many spectral visitors, and spate of unsolved modern day murders, one need look no further than the demonic past to throw some light on these macabre mysteries.

MR AND MRS PATRICK HENNESSY

WILTON CASTLE
County Wexford, Southern Ireland

THE SILHOUETTE of this spectacular castle is matched by the extraordinary and unearthly supernatural tales associated with it. The Alcock family lived at Wilton from 1695 until a year before the tragic fire that destroyed it in 1923. They had gone to live for a while in England leaving the castle in the hands of a caretaker but he was no match for the fanaticism of the IRA.

To learn more of the history and rumoured ghosts of Wilton I visited the local historian Patrick Hennessy and his wife, who live in a small thatched cottage close to one of the castle's driveways. I was immediately made welcome in true Irish style and sat entranced as Mr Hennessy began to tell me some remarkable stories as we sat around the fireplace. It appears that on the anniversary of the death of Harry Alcock, who died in 1840, a ghostly carriage would come down the castle driveway and crowds of locals would gather to see it. His ghost was also seen on the roads around the castle and a local shoemaker claimed to have actually spoken with it. Mrs Hennesssy told me that strange lights could sometimes be seen in a tower of the castle where an old woman, a one-time actress, had been burnt to death.

The strangest tale was kept till last, though. Mr Hennessy recounted the story of the notorious yeoman, Captain Archibald Jacob, who lived at Ballinapierce nearby. As well

as being captain of the Vinegar Hill Rangers he was a magistrate in Enniscorthy at the time of the 1798 Rebellion and was well known as a tyrant. He flogged and tortured many people in the parish and was universally disliked there. On 29 December, 1836, Captain Jacob was killed by a fall from his horse at a place called the Black Stream, between Wilton Castle and Clough Mills, after returning from a ball at the castle, and his spectre was said to then haunt this spot and the castle.

However, the then Lady Alcock, herself a Protestant, claimed it was the ghost of the local Catholic priest, Father Devereux, who had died around the same time and was suspected of being a hard drinker and gambler. Another young priest called Father Devereux, no relation, came to the parish and visited Wilton Castle to challenge Lady Alcock and to exorcise the house. On making the sign of the cross the ghost of Jacob appeared in the fireplace and then disappeared in a cloud of smoke.

KITTY'S STEPS
Lydford Gorge, Devon, England

A VERY ANCIENT superstition lingers on in the folklore of many lands, that of water-sprites or white ladies. The wraiths materialize from springs and waterfalls to entice a victim, a human sacrifice, to join them in their watery bowers. They have their origin in the Great White Goddess, Diana of the Moon, an ancient ruler over Nature. She would appear in many different forms and it is not hard to imagine why the tall and slender waterfall in the wild and beautiful Lydford Gorge is known as 'The White Lady'. But it is from the smaller, more secluded cascade known as 'Kitty's Steps' and the haunted pool below it, that the following story originates.

Many years ago, an old lady, who was simply known as Kitty, was returning home through the Gorge one summer evening. She was a creature of habit and would always take a short cut by passing through the ravine rather than keeping to the recognized path. This route took her past the waterfall, which she knew well, having often played there as a child. But she never returned home that night and several days later the red handkerchief that she always wore tied around her head was found near the pool. What exactly happened to her has never been explained. Some say she slipped and fell, others that she was beckoned by a supernatural force. On the anniversary of her death her ghost is said to appear near the waterfall, her head bowed, staring into the dark waters of the pool.

In 1968 a young soldier, who was in a hurry to return to his camp one night, took the same short cut across the Gorge. He was missing for several weeks despite an intensive search of the area. Some time later his body was found floating on the surface of the dark pool below 'Kitty's Steps'. A verdict of accidental death was brought in. The coroner made the following statement. 'He could have been overcome by the atmosphere of the Gorge, which I personally think is not a cheerful place even in the daytime. In the gloom and damp he may have been overcome by its eeriness and had a certain compulsion to jump in. But there is no evidence of premeditation.'

RAYNHAM HALL

Norfolk, England

THE 'Brown Lady' of Raynham Hall, ancestral home of the Marquess of Townshend, is considered to be one of England's 'classic' ghosts. She is described as appearing in a rich brown brocade dress, her hair in a coif, and her face lit by a strange light which illuminates her features to reveal dark hollows, reminiscent of the eyeless sockets of a skull. She is thought to be Dorothy Walpole, the sister of the famous statesman, Sir Robert Walpole. Her husband, Lord Charles Townshend, discovered that she was having an affair with a dissolute, Lord Wharton, and was so jealous and outraged that he imprisoned her in her quarters at the Hall, where she wasted away until her death in 1726: Another version of the story says that she was found at the foot of the grand staircase with her neck broken.

Her ghost has been seen many times over the years. At one point policemen had to be employed, disguised as servants, to calm the fears of the real staff and to try and discover whether there was a practical joker at work. They were unable to prove anything. A more drastic measure was

GHOST OF 'THE BROWN LADY' OF RAYNHAM HALL

employed by the novelist Captain Maryatt. While staying at the house he encountered her ghost, which 'glanced at him in a diabolical manner' in a corridor and he fired a pistol at her. The bullet passed through the apparition and was later found embedded in a door.

A famous photograph of the Brown Lady descending the

staircase was taken by the photographer, Captain Provand, while he was on assignment at the house for *Country Life* magazine in 1936. Several experts have examined the original photograph and can find no evidence of forgery.

I visited the Hall on a bitterly cold but sunny winter's day. Unfortunately the present owner was unable to talk to me as he already had visitors. Having gained his permission to photograph the exterior of the house I was immediately fascinated by the ray of light that shone upon the front, and could not help thinking back to what I had read previously about the strange light that is reputed to illuminate the Brown Lady's ghostly features when she appears.

WOLFETON HOUSE
Dorset, England

A CURIOUS legend is attached to the dining-room at Wolfeton House in Dorset. The house, a mixture of medieval and Elizabethan architecture, was in the possession of the Trenchard family until the early part of the last century. During the ownership of Sir Thomas Trenchard (1630-1657) one of the judges of the Assize came to dine at Wolfeton, but no sooner had the company sat down to eat than his Lordship, greatly to everyone's surprise, suddenly ordered his carriage and abruptly left the house. On the way back to Dorchester he told his marshall that he had seen, standing behind Lady Trenchard's chair, a figure of her Ladyship with her throat cut and her head

WOLFETON HOUSE

WOLFETON HOUSE

THE 'HAUNTED' DINING-ROOM

THE CEILING ABOVE THE MAIN STAIRCASE

under her arm. Before the carriage reached the town a messenger overtook it on horseback with the news that Lady Trenchard had just committed suicide. Her ghost still haunts the house, headless and dressed in grey.

There are other ghosts that haunt this beautiful house. A member of the Trenchard family has been seen driving a ghostly coach-and-horses up the main staircase and it is said that whilst alive he once won a wager performing this eccentric feat. The spectre of a Catholic priest has been seen in the medieval gatehouse where he was imprisoned before being hanged, drawn and quartered in nearby Dorchester.

BETTISCOMBE MANOR
Dorset, England

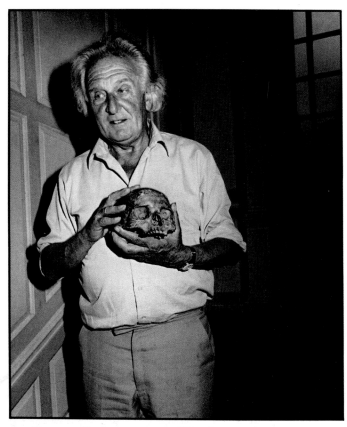

MICHAEL PINNEY HOLDING 'THE SCREAMING SKULL OF
BETTISCOMBE MANOR'

HIDDEN away in Marshwood Vale in Dorset lies historic Bettiscombe Manor or, as it is otherwise known, 'The House of the Screaming Skull'. The Pinney family have lived here for many centuries and it is around one of their number, a young man named Azariah, that the legend of the skull was born.

In 1685 Azariah joined the ill-fated Duke of Monmouth's forces during the rebellion of that year. After the Duke's defeat Azariah was sentenced to death by the infamous Judge Jeffreys at the Bloody Assizes. He won a reprieve but was banished to the West Indies as a free man, where he quickly began to prosper in business on the Island of Nevis. Some years later he decided to return to England, bringing with him his faithful negro slave. But the slave grew homesick, and was eyed with great suspicion by the locals, some of whom had never seen a black man before. The climate was also foreign to him and after a short time he died of consumption. On the eve of the slave's death he vowed that his spirit would not rest until his body was returned to his native land but Azariah did not feel it practical to carry out his final wish and had him buried in the local churchyard.

The slave would not rest below ground. Terrible screams were heard from the grave, the doors and windows in the house slammed and rattled, and several of the farm animals died mysteriously. To try and stop these disturbances the body was dug up and in the process the skull became separated from the rest of the body. Whether the body was shipped back to the West Indies is unclear but the skull remained in the manor. The poltergeist activities ceased and all was calm until some years later a tenant of the manor decided to dispose of the grisly relic by throwing it into a pond on the estate.

A demonic screaming shattered the peace of the vale and the disturbances were so bad that the man was forced to wade into the pool to retrieve it. Ever since the skull is said to have reacted in the same way if it has been taken out of the house. At one point it was said to have been buried nine feet deep but slowly rose to the surface of the ground of its own accord, and in 1914 it is reported to have sweated blood.

When I visited Bettiscombe I found Michael Pinney sitting in the kitchen reading an ancient book of folklore. He was very intelligent and sympathetic, serving me one of the most delicious English teas I have ever tasted. He then showed me the skull, which he keeps in an old cardboard box, and would naturally never dream of taking outside the house. During our conversation he told me that although he did not totally disregard the legend he did feel that the skull could have been a 'luck' for the Pinney family which protected the house from ghosts and evil spirits.

He explained that behind the house was a steep hill called Pilsdon Pen, a very ancient and sacred site used as a Celtic place of worship. The Celts were headhunters and would pickle their victim's skulls in honey carrying them into battle in wooden boxes believing that all power derived from the human skull. Perhaps the Bettiscombe skull has its origins in these archaic customs, but whether the skull is that of a negro slave or an ancient Briton, the experience of holding it in my hands was singularly eerie.

CASTLE GRANT
Morayshire, Scotland

BARBARA Grant, the daughter of a sixteenth-century Grant chieftain, was ordered by her father to marry a man from another clan whom she did not love. When she refused to obey his orders he had her locked in a cupboard where she was left to starve to death unless she changed her mind. She chose death, and it is her small and benevolent ghost that haunts the tower, known as Babette's tower, to this day.

A macabre relic, a skull of one of the Comyns, former owners of the castle, is still preserved in the castle as a 'luck'. The cranium is hinged and it contains a number of secret documents. There is a legendary curse on the relic: if it should pass out of the family they would lose all their property in Strathspey. The skull is said to be kept in the castle vaults and was last seen by a kitchen maid working at the castle before the Grants moved out forty years ago.

Another legend tells of a piper who came down from Inverness with news of the Clan's defeat at the battle of Culloden. It is said that he piped twice around the castle but on the third circuit he dropped dead. A cross on the side of the castle commemorates this, but his ghost can still be seen trying to complete his task.

While I was having a cup of tea in the kitchens one of the workmen involved in renovating the castle told me that he had twice seen, in his own words, a 'trace' spirit which he described as somebody who had done the same thing many times in their life and therefore leaves an 'impression'. In this particular case it was a serving maid who appeared to be passing dishes to someone. He had seen the spirit in broad daylight several times in the dining-room of the castle.

ARDOGINNA HOUSE
County Waterford, Southern Ireland

MY first impression, standing amid the remains of this sinister and uncanny Gothic ruin, was of being in a foreign country, perhaps Spain or Mexico, certainly not on the wild Irish coastline. As I surveyed the gnarled and windswept trees that once proudly sheltered the now broken Moorish walls I could not help but wonder what secrets lay hidden in the fragmented stones of this strange house.

The earliest history of 'Ardo' is vague but it was inhabited in the seventeenth century by a family called Costen. The young heir was tricked by his guardian and branded a thief. Pursued by soldiers along the cliffs near the house he tried to jump a ravine and was hung by his own horse's reins. The spot to this day is known as 'Crook-an-Heire' or 'The Gallows of the Heir'. The place is said to be haunted and unearthly screams can be heard above the roar of the sea below.

The house passed briefly to the Prendergasts when another crime was committed. Sir Francis Prendergast is said to have had one of his servants, who offended him, secretly hanged from a beam in the ceiling of one of the rooms. This caused much supernatural activity and when the old house was pulled down a skeleton, believed to be that of the servant, was found beneath the dining-room floor.

The Coghlans obtained possession of 'Ardo' in the early part of the eighteenth century. 'Madam' Coghlan, as she was known, supported her family's extravagant and reckless life-style by helping the smugglers that frequented the coast. She and her husband, Jeremiah, had four children; two beautiful daughters who made successful marriages, and two idiot children, Thomasina, a hunchback who still played with her dolls at the age of eighty-five, and Jeremiah, who carried his favourite kittens in his pockets wherever he went. They both died in loneliness and poverty. It was 'Madam' Coghlan who turned 'Ardo' into a fantasy house but inevitably the family was destined for financial ruin. The house by now was considered to be both unlucky and horribly haunted. Among the many stories at this time was one of a dangerous loose step on the main staircase that would never stay in place ever since a child's body had been discovered beneath it.

The last owners of the fateful house were the McKennas, who would seem to have led a far more peaceful existence there than their predecessors, although they are said to have seen the ghost of Jeremiah Coghlan riding his horse on the roads near the house, carrying a crimson banner in honour of the marriage of one of his beautiful daughters.

On my way back from the ruin which, as night was beginning to fall, I was not sorry to be leaving, I stumbled by chance across an overgrown statue guarding the McKennas' mausoleum which provided just one more macabre touch. The inscription read:

My life is like a broken stair,
Winding round a ruined tower,
And leading nowhere.

[63]

BERRY POMEROY CASTLE

Devon, England

SURROUNDED by massive beech trees, this rambling and ruined castle lies close to the edge of a steep cliff. The castle was originally built by the powerful de la Pomerai family, who lived there from the Norman Conquest until the mid-sixteenth century, over 500 years of uninterrupted succession. After the religious rebellion of 1549 all strongholds of those who had joined the uprising were ordered to be demolished, but the two Pomeroy brothers who held the castle, having enjoyed centuries of power, were unwilling to bow to the command of the distant boy king, Edward VI, or rather that of his Protector, Edward Seymour. As the besieging army surrounded the castle the two knights are said to have hidden all their family treasure, blindfolded their chargers and in full regalia rode over the ramparts, hurtling to their deaths in the valley below. The King's officials confiscated the castle and sold it to the Seymour family, who spent £20,000 building an elaborate mansion within the precincts of the old walls. This now stands gaunt and gutted, after being struck by lightning and set on fire in 1685.

The acts of cruelty and violence that have taken place at Berry Pomeroy over the ages have given rise to several ghost stories. One of these concerns two sisters, Eleanor and Margaret Pomeroy. Eleanor was plain and ungainly, but Margaret was beautiful beyond compare. It was fated that they should both fall in love with the same man. Eleanor, the elder of the two, was so jealous of her sister's beauty that she used her power as mistress of the castle to keep her locked in a dungeon beneath one of the towers. As Margaret slowly starved to death in her dark and lonely vault, the evil Eleanor enjoyed the company of the man who had by now become her lover and sometimes in the middle of the night she would visit her dying sister and describe to her the intimacies of their lovemaking at the same time delighting in the sight of her sister's withering beauty.

Eventually death released Margaret from her terrible ordeal, but her ghost came back to haunt her sister. Now, on certain nights of the year, she is said to arise from her entombed dungeon, leave St Margaret's Tower and walk along the ramparts in a long white flowing robe, beckoning to any beholder to come and join her in the dungeon below. It is said that, if anyone sees her, they will go insane and die shortly afterwards.

ST MICHAEL'S MOUNT

Cornwall, England

AT ONE time a large forest covered the coast around St Michael's Mount, hence the ancient Cornish name for it is 'Carreg luz en kuz', meaning 'the white rock in the wood'. It was known to be an important place of Druidical worship. Before Christianity reached these shores there were many legends of giants connected with the Mount and one of these explains how it supposedly came into existence.

It is said that the Giant Cormoran wished to build his home here, raised above the trees so that he could keep watch over his rivals in the neighbouring countryside. He selected the white granite rocks from the surrounding hills and with the help of his wife, Cornellian, carried them back to the site. She tired of searching further and further afield for the white rock her husband preferred and so began to collect instead the nearby greenstones, carrying them in her apron. When Cormoran discovered this he followed her and in his anger gave her a great kick. The apron strings broke and a stone fell into the sand. No human power has been able to move it from where it landed. I was unable to confirm whether this was the stone in the foreground of the photograph.

The St Aubyn family have lived at the Mount since 1659 and despite its varied and torrid history the only reported ghost is that of a tall and confused figure that haunts the Priory Church on the Mount. During the last century renovation work in the church revealed a small dungeon reached by a stone stair. Inside the cell was the skeleton of a man over seven feet tall. The entrance is now hidden by the family pews.

BUCHANNAN CASTLE
Stirlingshire, Scotland

THIS awesome and derelict nineteenth-century ruin is now surrounded by an estate of modern houses that give it an even more unreal 'magnetism'. During the last war it was the temporary prison of Rudolf Hess, Hitler's deputy leader.

The castle is reputed to be haunted by strange groans and whimperings that have been heard by local people late at night. The lady that I interviewed said that she no longer walked her dog around the castle during the day or night as it simply refused to go near it. The noises are said to be loud and incessant and they have been heard by many impartial and reliable witnesses.

The sheer size and appearance of the castle inspired in me a vision of an immense 'ghost ship' slowly passing in the night, containing any number of nightmares one's imagination might allow itself to realize.

THE HAUNTING OF
BORLEY RECTORY
Essex, England

THE Domesday Book records that there was a monastery in the quiet hamlet of Borley as long ago as the thirteenth century. According to a local legend one of the monks from the monastery fell in love with a young nun from the nearby convent in Bures. At a secret lover's tryst they planned to elope together, but their plan was discovered, and they were both condemned for their transgression. The monk met his fate on the gallows and the nun was sentenced to be bricked up alive in the cellars of the monastery.

Through the following centuries villagers began to report sightings of a mysterious woman 'floating' over the grounds of the ruined monastery and the adjoining churchyard. Then in 1863 the rector of Borley, the Reverend Henry Bull, decided to build a new rectory on the site of the ancient monastery. It was shortly after this that the events took place which earned this house its reputation as 'the most haunted house in England'.

The Reverend Henry Bull, and his son Harry who succeeded him, both saw the ghost of the nun many times, always remarking on her sad and mournful expression. The

Bulls' servants would frequently leave, claiming to have seen the nun and other apparitions, including a spectral coach; and on one occasion Harry's four sisters all witnessed the nun floating across the front lawn in broad daylight.

In 1927 Harry Bull died and the incumbency passed to the Reverend Eric Smith and his wife. Warned about stories of the rectory being haunted they decided to call in Harry Price, the celebrated psychic researcher. His arrival at the rectory was greeted with a ferocious outburst of poltergeist activity. Objects were unaccountably smashed and stones were 'hurled' at him. All this proved too much for the Smiths and they decided to leave.

Six months later the new rector, the Reverend Lionel Foyster and his family, arrived. The unaccountable phenomena now took a more violent form, focusing for the most part on the rector's young wife, Marianne. Objects were frequently 'thrown' at her, inexplicable phenomena 'materialized' from nowhere and messages were scribbled on the rectory walls. Many of these scribblings were illegible, but some of them contained distinct messages, 'pleas for help and prayers'. Several of these messages even 'appeared' in the presence of witnesses.

HARRY PRICE (1881–1948)

Driven to distraction the Reverend Lionel Foyster decided that the house should be exorcised. As a result the manifestations ceased. But it was not long before new manifestations began. At odd hours weird music would emanate from the empty church, communion wine would mysteriously turn into ink, bells in the house would begin ringing of their own accord, and finally the Foyster's child was the victim of a strange incident. According to the child it was attacked by 'something horrible'. This was the last straw, and the Foysters at once left — whereupon the rectory remained empty, for no new incumbent would live in it.

Intrigued by all these further reports, Harry Price decided to rent the rectory, and moved in in 1937. He advertised in *The Times* for trustworthy helpers and began a prolonged investigation. On 27 March 1938, during a seance held by some of his assistants, a communicator calling himself 'Sunex Amures' claimed that the rectory would burn down that very night. He told them that a fire would start in the hall, and that the remains of a nun would be discovered under the ruins of the rectory. But despite this curious warning, nothing happened.

Later that year Harry Price's tenancy expired and the rectory was bought by a Captain Gregson. Immediately upon taking up residence he began experiencing all kinds

BORLEY RECTORY (BEFORE THE FIRE)

PSYCHIC 'WALL WRITINGS', BORLEY RECTORY

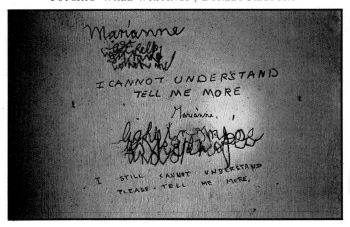

of inexplicable occurrences, including the mysterious disappearance of his two dogs. Then on the evening of 27 February 1939, preciecly eleven months to the day after the mysterious warning at the seance, the rectory burnt down. The fire was started by an oil lamp, which fell over for no apparent reason. In the midst of the furious conflagration several onlookers noticed strange figures moving amid the smoke and flames and then they saw the cowled figure of a nun at an upstairs window.

By now the haunted house had become a *cause célèbre*,

THE CHURCHYARD, BORLEY

and in 1943 Harry Price and several helpers returned to the ruins to begin further investigations. Excavating beneath the cellars they discovered the skeleton of a young woman. These remains were finally given a Christian burial. However, to this day, the figure of a nun is still reported to haunt the site of the rectory and nearby churchyard.

Of all the sites I visited during the making of this book Borley remains the most frightening and intriguing. On my first visit I took two great friends with me who were both very sceptical of the existence of ghosts but neither could wait to leave after a very short time. The whole area looked and felt very 'haunted' although it has recently been somewhat modernized, and there is virtually nothing left of the original rectory. The photograph of the churchyard includes a 'shape' in the sky that I have never been able to explain although I do all my own printing and developing. During my research I have come across several articles where other photographers have had similar experiences at Borley.

[71]

HAVERHOLME PRIORY

Lincolnshire, England

IT IS SAID that Charles Dickens used Haverholme Priory in Lincolnshire as his model for Chesney Wold in *Bleak House*.

The ghost here is well documented in Lord Halifax's famous *Ghost Book* first published in 1936. It appears that a Mr H W Hill, the then secretary of the English Church Union, stayed at the priory in 1905 as the tenants were old friends of his. On the night of his arrival, having conversed with his hosts, he was eventually shown to his room in a tower in the old part of the house. It was around midnight when he undressed and got into bed but after a short while he heard footsteps walking unceasingly up and down the gravelled path underneath his window. He thought little of this at the time and slowly drifted off to sleep.

The next morning he enquired of the son of the house who might have been pacing up and down the path so late at night, only to be told that everybody else in the house had retired at the same time as himself and that all the doors had been securely locked. At dinner the following evening Mr Hill met a Miss Antrobus, who informed him that Haverholme had been built on the site of a Gilbertine priory, and that the path running below his bedroom was known as the 'Ghost Walk' and that footsteps could frequently be heard pacing along it.

On another of Mr Hill's visits to Haverholme, a year later, he experienced the strange 'whizzing' noise that occurs at a bridge in the grounds of the priory at the end of a long avenue of elm trees. Horses and dogs become terrified at this spot and both the avenue and bridge are said to be haunted by a Gilbertine canoness.

When I visited the priory and grounds there was little left of the overgrown ruins to see. I spoke to a man who let me take photographs but did not seem keen to talk of the ghost although he knew of the stories and pointed out that Thomas à Becket had once taken refuge at the priory. The area had a very 'ancient' feel about it but I neither saw nor heard anything unusual that evening.

'Haunted Bridge', Haverholme Priory
Lord Halifax (1839–1934)

CREECH HILL

Somerset, England

NOT FAR from Bruton, on the summit of Creech Hill, lies the site of a Romano-Celtic temple. Several excavations have been carried out here and during one of these, in the late eighteenth century, two crossed bodies were found, believed to be Norman and Saxon. The hill and the wasteland below it have had an evil reputation for many years. Late at night passers by have heard following footsteps and strange laughter and the locals tell stories of a gruesome black shape that haunts the hill.

It is said that one night a farmer, who was returning from a nearby market, came across something lying in the road at the foot of the hill. Fearing that it was somebody who was hurt he went to offer help. As he approached the figure rose up to an eerie height letting out a fearful screech. The farmer fled, his uncanny pursuer keeping close behind him, until finally he reached his own house. His wife, alarmed by his cries for help, rushed to the door to discover what had happened. As she tried to comfort him she caught sight of a long black figure bounding back towards Creech Hill emitting a shriek of laughter as it disappeared.

Another account, told by a housemaid from Bruton, relates how a very staid and sober gentleman had a pressing engagement one night that left him with no alternative but to cross over the hill. Knowing of its reputation he armed himself with a lantern and a stout hazel stick. He set out at a brisk pace and it was not until he was halfway over the hill that he became aware of a deadly coldness. Suddenly something tall and black rose out of the ground in front of him. He struck wildly at it with his staff, but the stick went straight through his tormentor and he found that he was transfixed to the spot. Peals of crazy laughter deafened him at every desperate stroke that he made and he was unable to free himself until he heard a distant cock crow and suddenly he was alone on the hill in the first pale light of dawn. For a moment he looked around him but the hideous shape had vanished. He wondered whether it had all been a terrible nightmare, then he suddenly remembered his appointment. He took a couple of steps forward but fainted dead away.

Several hours later he was found by two ploughmen. They carried him back to the safety of his home where he remained desperately ill for many weeks. He never really recovered from his horrific ordeal and his neighbours told how he would spend many hours staring out of his window towards the hill as if something were beckoning to him to join it there.

Snow lay thick on the ground when I climbed the hill. I had to pass by a present day maggot factory which lent one more macabre touch to the scene. A strange mist hung around the trees on the summit and I was content to approach just close enough to take this photograph.

DUNTROON CASTLE

Argyllshire, Scotland

ALTHOUGH now owned by the Malcolm family this castle, dominating a rocky promontory on the north side of Loch Crinan, formerly belonged to the Campbells in the seventeenth century. At this time a rival chieftain known as 'Left-handed Coll Macdonnell' had a personal score to settle with the Campbells of Duntroon and having ravaged their lands sent out his personal piper to spy on the castle. The disguised piper was welcomed by the Campbells and in turn he entertained his hosts. Several days passed and his inordinate interest in the castle's defences aroused the Campbells' suspicion and so they imprisoned him in a turret room.

Now desperate to warn his clansmen that the castle was virtually impregnable and that the Campbells were on their guard, the piper began to play a famous tune now known as 'The piper's warning to his Master'. The warning was heeded and 'Coll' turned back, but in their rage the Campbells cut off the piper's hands, and he died from the shock and loss of blood.

When we visited the Castle on a misty summer's evening the present day Malcolms told us that when restoration work was being carried out at the castle a handless skeleton was discovered under the cellar floor and that the piper's tunes can still sometimes be heard in the castle.

THORNTON ABBEY
Lincolnshire, England

THE abbey was founded in 1139 by William le Gros and the imposing gatehouse is said to be one of the finest examples of such a structure in Britain. The remote setting of the abbey means that facts about its history are scarce but it is known that the gatehouse was fortified in 1382 at the time of a peasants' uprising in Lincolnshire.

That the abbey contained great wealth is without doubt, but what strikes the visitor most are the ghastly and terrifying gargoyles that watch one from both inside and outside the huge gatehouse. Some of these are carved in stone, others in wood, and include bats, beasts and human heads. Entering through the massive wooden doors, one could quickly believe that one had stumbled into the depths of hell.

This was one of the places where I truly felt frightened on my travels; a strange sort of fear, as if I had been here before, either in this life or a previous one. As I was born in Lincolnshire the former is possible, but my parents denied ever taking me there as a child.

It was with no surprise then that I learnt of the phantom that still haunts the abbey. According to ancient documents or writings now kept in the Bodleian Library, the fourteenth Abbot of Thornton, Thomas de Gretham, was believed to have been involved in witchcraft and black magic or more

GARGOYLE, THORNTON ABBEY

likely to have succumbed to the sins of the flesh or both. For his crimes he was bricked up alive in a dungeon off the chapter-house. Several centuries later, when some workmen were taking down a wall in the abbey, they came upon the skeletal form of a man together with a table, candlestick and book. When one of the men touched the figure it crumbled to dust.

[79]

DUCKETTS GROVE

County Carlow, Southern Ireland

THE grounds of Ducketts Grove are entered through the most stupendous castellated gateway in Southern Ireland, until recently used as a lounge bar. The Ducketts, a wealthy English family, lived here from 1830 until 1912. The house was accidentally burned down in 1933. The estate covered many acres and the following description of the house and grounds is taken from an article in a local journal, *The Ducketts and Ducketts Grove*, by Mrs Mary Pender:

Hanging in the portico was something in the style of a glass chandelier which tinkled and sounded like Fairy Music when the hall door was opened. Numerous statuettes, male and female, lined both sides of the avenue

described to me. Miss Brady surrounds herself with animals of all descriptions; wolfhounds, horses, dogs, cats, chickens, the numbers seem endless. Local children help her to look after the animals. As we sat having tea in what was once the regal courtyard of the house, Miss Brady told us of the 'ghostly music' that she had heard at the castle and which seemed to emanate from the very walls themselves. She says that the music has a sad and plaintive melody and is played on either an organ or harmonium. She had heard it both during the day and at night.

A local legend says that in the eighteenth century one of the daughters of the house fell in love with a musician but her parents disapproved of the match and she died of a broken heart. It is said that her lover still serenades her. Local people also say that the music was even heard by intruders when the house lay empty and abandoned after the fire of 1933.

In her article Mary Pender refers to music played at Quaker meetings (the Ducketts were believed to have been Quakers) which were held in front of the mansion in the early years of this century. She recalls: 'Old people of the district distinctly remember hearing the singing and the music of a harmonium at evening time'.

As we left Miss Brady invited us to return on the night of Hallowe'en when the children dress up as ghosts and act out a play they have written about the house. Perhaps, she said, I would like to make a film of it?

in front of the mansion. Carved heads both human and animal adorned the outside walls. A weeping ash tree to the front of the main hall door housed a stately seated lady who, according to old people, inquired your business when you entered the summerhouse formed by the weeping ash.

The Gothic architecture adds to the ghostly feel of the house which the very hospitable owner, Frances Brady, later

BARBRECK HOUSE
Argyllshire, Scotland

THIS house once belonged to the Campbells but is now owned by a Mrs Hayes who rents it out while still living nearby. There is an ancient burial vault to the Campbells in the grounds containing several memorial plaques to clan members. An ancient stone circle lies behind the house. The beautiful estate of moors, lochs and rivers is haunted by the ghost of a 'hooded' maiden with long hair and a very pale, sad face. She wears an undetermined plaid or tartan and has been sighted by many local shepherds and fishermen. She is usually seen seated on a rock near Loch Craignish and always disappears when approached. Who she was, who she grieves or waits for and why, nobody knows.

The Campbells were considered traitors during the time of the Highland Uprisings and the house was used as an English garrison to suppress local resistance. Perhaps this turbulent period of Scotland's history could provide the answer to the source of this young girl's sorrow.

When I was photographing the house I met a local man collecting milk. I asked him where I could find the Campbells' burial ground but he curtly replied, 'The graveyard is the only fit place for them,' and hurriedly walked away.

DUNSTAFFGNE CASTLE
Argyllshire, Scotland

THIS thirteenth-century castle stands on a rocky promontory at the entrance of Loch Etive near Oban. The original sixth-century castle was believed to have been the seat of the Dalriadic Government and to have housed the famous 'Stone of Scone' or 'Destiny' thought to have been the pillow of Jacob when he dreamed of a ladder to heaven. It became the coronation stone of the kings of Scotland and latterly England and is now kept in Westminster Abbey.

The castle became a Campbell stronghold from 1308, when captured from the MacDougalls of Lorn, until it was finally destroyed by fire in 1810. It is haunted by a heavy footed ghost known as the 'Ell-Maid of Dunstaffgne'. This lady is dressed in green and her appearance is always preceded by intense poltergeist activity. Her materialization heralds either great joy or sadness, but her identity remains a mystery. Another ghost that has been seen here is that of Flora MacDonald, Bonnie Prince Charlie's rescuer after his defeat at Culloden; she was imprisoned here for a time in 1746.

Huntingdon Castle

County Carlow, Southern Ireland

THE CASTLE is approached through a long avenue of lime trees. Originally built in 1625, it stands somewhat severe and aloof, but its appearance gave me little warning of the strange experiences in the realm of ghosts and pure eccentricity that I was about to undergo.

We were met at the door by Olivia Durdin-Robertson whose family have lived at the castle for over 200 years. She told me how delighted she was to see a stranger as the day was beginning to look rather boring. Perhaps we would like to stay to lunch?

Olivia, a very enthusiastic and amusing guide, gave us a preliminary tour around the house which is a veritable memorial to times gone by. There are endless dark and forbidding corridors, and rooms crammed with tapestries, family portraits, suits of chain-mail, dusty old books, stuffed crocodiles and buffalo heads. It was as if they were living in a continuous 'twilight world' where time had stood still. At this point Olivia's sixty-five year old brother Lawrence appeared, a quiet enchanting man, who had resigned his post as a clergyman in Norfolk, calling himself Baron Strethlock. He has been registered as such by the Chief Herald of Ireland although Strethlock is in Scotland.

The Durdin-Robertsons founded the Fellowship of Isis, a cult dedicated to the Egyptian Goddess Isis and just about any other Goddess one should wish to worship. To be in the service of the Goddess is to seek perfect freedom, in short the 'Truth'. To reach this end one must achieve 'balance' in one's life and rid oneself of all guilt, including sexual guilt and the guilt of owning material goods. The Fellowship has over 6000 members from all over the world which number several famous people, such as the South American novelist, Jorge Luis Borges. They often entertain witches from other countries at their various ceremonies which take place in the Temple, in the castle dungeons.

Olivia began to talk of the ghosts at Huntingdon, which are legion. She said that occultism runs in the family and that all ghosts are welcome here. She then took us out into the grounds to show us the mysterious 600-year-old Yew Walk where an ancient ancestor can often be seen walking in deep meditation. Other ghosts in the gardens include a spectral dogcart that comes up the avenue of

THE YEW WALK, HUNTINGDON CASTLE

HUNTINGDON CASTLE

OLIVIA AND LAWRENCE DURDIN-ROBERTSON

lime trees, and Grace O'Malley, the legendary 'Pirate Queen', who appears at the 'Spy Bush' combing her hair by the light of the moon.

Later, during lunch, Olivia opened a vintage bottle of wine and began to talk of the phantoms who inhabit the house. She pointed to an ancient portrait above my head of Barbara St Leger of Doneraile Court in County Cork, who had married into the family. The St Legers were a famous hunting family, although the fourth Viscount Doneraile, perhaps the most famous huntsman of his day, ironically died of rabies after being bitten by a pet fox. Barbara St Leger's ghost is reputed to walk up and down the chapel, her keys tied around her waist. Barbara's maid, Honor Byrne, is also a ghost here and she can be seen in the chapel passage rubbing down doors with her hair.

A ghostly hand has also been seen. Lawrence's daughter Melian felt it when sleeping in the Yellow Room. She said it was very small and cold and played with her hand and then squeezed it tightly. A drunken soldier has been heard banging on the door at midnight. Olivia says that he must have been locked out in the seventeenth century. At this moment a trolley bearing food suddenly shot out of the fireplace. On closer inspection the fireplace turned out to be the serving hatch from the kitchen.

Other ghosts include an Edwardian nurse seen in the Red Room, and an eighteenth-century gentleman in white wig and costume who inspects new guests in this room, probably the last night they spend there. These particular ghosts are strays, says Olivia. They come and go as they please as there is a rapport between the living and the so-called dead at the castle.

After lunch Lawrence and Olivia changed into ceremonial clothes so that I could photograph them in the Temple. They both wore long robes, Olivia clutching a wand. The Temple itself has many alcoves, each dedicated to a different Goddess, containing strange relics and statues from many different cultures. There is also a well containing magic water which is used in the ceremonies.

When it was time to leave, the Durdin-Robertsons, still in their ceremonial robes, escorted us to our car. Outside in the courtyard we passed what Olivia described

[86]

as an ancient masonic stone pillar with a stone ball on top, rather like a human head. She told me that she recently returned to the house late one night to find a local man deep in conversation with it.

I was so inspired by their generous hospitality, eccen-

tricity and peculiar stories that I could only reflect that these things were something to be protected in our modern day mechanical world. In my eyes at least I believed that my hosts had attained their goal and could truly be described as 'free spirits'.

THE MANOR OF RILLATON

Bodmin Moor, Cornwall, England

SINCE earliest times a story has been passed down about the ghost of a Druid priest who used to haunt the prehistoric burial mound in the Manor of Rillaton on Bodmin Moor. According to the legend the Druidic phantom would waylay lone passers by, offering them a golden cup containing a magic potion, which could never be drained.

Late one night a nobleman of the district was returning home after a hard day's hunting on the moor. It had been a good day's sport and the nobleman had celebrated with his fellow hunters well into the night at a nearby inn. Though a little the worse for wear after his revels the nobleman insisted on returning home. As he rode past the ancient burial mound near the prehistoric stones known as the Cheesewring he thought he saw a figure approaching him from out of the mists. Reining up his horse he made out a frail old man dressed in a long robe clasping a gold cup in his hands.

elements could do no harm. Snatching up the cup from the expressionless stranger he took a a quick draught. The liquid tasted sweet and on impulse the nobleman drained the cup, all the while watching the mysterious robed figure out of the corner of his eye. But when he lowered the cup he was surprised to see that some dregs still remained. Raising the cup to his lips, he drained it once more — only to find that yet again some liquid remained.

'What trickery is this?' he demanded. But still the mysterious stranger remained silent. In an access of drunken rage the nobleman tossed the dregs into the stranger's face and threw the cup at his feet. But the stranger still stood there, motionless and silent the dregs running down his cheeks like tears, yet with a strange sardonic smile appearing to enliven his features. Digging his spurs into his horse, the nobeman galloped off into the night without daring to look behind him — the image of the stranger's mysterious smile imprinted on his mind.

When the nobleman arrived home and told his tale, the locals reminded him of the ancient story. But what did this meeting with the mysterious figure portend, he wondered? What did it mean? A few days later, the body of the nobleman and his horse were found dead at the bottom of a nearby ravine.

Years later, in 1837, archaeologists began a series of excavations in the Manor of Rillaton. Whilst digging in the prehistoric mound, which is now known as 'Rillaton Barrow', a skeleton was unearthed, and beside it a gold beaker dating from 1500 BC. The beaker was presented to King William IV who for a while used it as his shaving mug. Later the beaker came into the possession of the British Museum, where it is still on display to this day.

THE CHEESEWRING, BODMIN MOOR

THE 'RILLATON CUP'

As the robed figure approached the nobleman saw that the old man's complexion was pallid and his eyes had a strangely vacant stare. Without a word the robed figure held up the cup in his outstretched hands as if offering the nobleman a drink. Slightly suspicious of this strange apparition the nobleman asked him how such a valuable vessel had come into his possession and what it contained. But the robed figure remained silent, his outstretched hands seeming to implore him to drink. The nobleman felt a chill run through his body — but emboldened by his revels decided that a further drink to fortify him against the

CORBY CASTLE

Cumberland, England

PERHAPS the best known ghost in north-west England is the 'Radiant Boy' of Corby Castle. This luminous apparition takes the form of a beautiful boy clothed in white with golden shining hair. His appearances are rare and who he was, and whether or not he was a murder victim at the castle, is not known.

The castle, which was remodelled in the nineteenth century, stands on the bank of the River Eden. It incorporates a fourteenth-century pele-tower, and is the family seat of the Howards. The celebrated grounds include a spectacular 'cascade' that takes water from the parks down to the river below, and several impressive statues.

The 'Radiant Boy' usually appears in the 'ghost room' at the castle which was described in days gone by as being in the old part of the house, which has walls eight to ten feet thick and can only be reached by a passageway. The room itself was covered by tapestries and family portraits and contained other 'dark' and 'old fashioned' furniture

including some bizarre carved wooden figures. In short it had a gloomy and ominous atmosphere and people were wary of sleeping there.

The ghost has been seen by members of the Howard family on several occasions and in different locations, but it is the visitation at Corby described by Mrs Crowe in her often quoted book *The Night Side of Nature*, published in 1848, that gives us the most complete account of this phenomenon. It was witnessed by the Reverend Henry Redburgh, Rector of Greystoke, and his wife, who were staying at the castle in the autumn of 1803 and this extract is quoted from the journal of a member of the Howard family:

Soon after we went to bed we fell asleep; it might be between one and two in the morning when I awoke. I observed that the fire was totally extinguished; but although that was the case and we had no light, I saw a

THE 'RADIANT BOY' APPEARING TO LORD CASTLEREAGH,
IN IRELAND, C. 1800

glimmer in the centre of the room which suddenly increased to a bright flame. I looked out, apprehending that something had caught fire; when to my amazement, I beheld a beautiful boy, clothed in white, with bright locks resembling gold, standing by my bedside, in which position he remained some minutes, fixing his eyes upon me with a mild and benevolent expression. He then glided gently towards the side of the chimney where it is obvious there is no possible egress, and entirely disappeared. I found myself in total darkness and all remained quiet until the usual hour of rising. I declare this to be a true account of what I saw at Corby Castle, upon my word as a clergyman.

The Rector and his wife left the castle soon after breakfast the next day, never to return.

According to tradition the appearance of the 'Radiant Boy' heralds a rise to great fame and fortune, followed by violent death for the beholder. This does not seem to have befallen the Rector, who died peacefully in his sleep, but perhaps the explanation for this was that he was not a member of the Howard family.

One of their number, Captain Robert Stewart, later Lord Castlereagh and a War Minister in Pitt's cabinet, saw the 'Radiant Boy' when he was an unknown Captain in the army staying in a hunting party in Northern Ireland. He then reached great heights as a politician, but eventually began to slowly lose his mind, finally committing suicide by cutting his throat with a penknife at his home in North Cray Place in 1822.

CRAWFORD PRIORY

Fife, Scotland

THAT all hauntings are malevolent is an all too common assumption but, as in the rest of life, it would appear that it is evil rather than good that obsesses us anyway. However, there are many accounts of benign ghosts.

Lady Mary Lindsay Crawford, who built this ecclesiastical Gothic fantasy in 1813, was a great beauty of her time, an eccentric and a lover of animals. It is her benign spirit which is now reputed to haunt this deserted priory. It is said that her ghost can be seen wandering through the grounds gesticulating to unseen accomplices to follow her on her seemingly endless journey.

In those times to be a woman of independence, to stay unmarried and to live in virtual seclusion was to invite rumour, gossip and innuendo. However, Lady Mary decided to deny herself the love and company of a husband and to devote herself entirely to her entourage of dumb favourites. Among her legion of animals were dogs, birds, a tame fox, a deer and her brother's favourite charger. In her will she left instructions as to how this horse should be put to death; it was to be shot in its sleep so as to cause it the least amount of pain possible.

Not surprisingly Lady Mary was said to have high spirits and showed a quick temper with people who displeased her, but she was loved by all her servants. Her funeral, which took place in the Gothic hall of the priory in 1833, was witnessed by the twenty-fifth Earl of Crawford. He describes how, at the middle point of the service, the sun's rays streamed through the glass windows, lighting up the many suits of armour in the niches around the walls and the very death mask of Lady Mary, then faded away again. When the service was over the procession moved up a winding road to the family mausoleum at the top of a nearby hill. Many people came to watch and the Earl of Crawford said that he had never witnessed a more impressive scene.

When I last visited the priory in the summer of 1984 I gained permission to take photographs from a lady in the lodge, who telephoned the absent owner. I was greatly moved by the place; it seemed to me to be the perfect setting for a Gothic horror novel. It was with some surprise then that I later discovered the nature of the 'haunting', and I have to admit to being somewhat disappointed as I had expected, or perhaps desired, something far more horrific to have taken place there.

Hunstanton Hall
Norfolk, England

DAME Armine le Strange was married to Henry Styleman and, on the death of her brother Sir Robert le Strange in 1762, she inherited Hunstanton Hall. The le Strange family had lived at the hall for many years and she wished to continue the line through her eldest son, Nicholas. Nicholas Styleman, or 'The Jolly Gentleman' as he was known throughout the county of Norfolk, was a kind and generous man but an inveterate socializer and gambler. This combination of excesses caused him to sell many of the estate's treasures, even the herd of deer in the park, much to the horror and sadness of his mother. One of her favourite possessions was a large Persian carpet given to her by the Shah of Persia which incorporated an ancient poem in its design and in 1766, as Dame Armine lay dying in her ravaged home, she summoned her son to her bedside and made him swear that he would never sell or dispose of the carpet. If he or anybody else should do so she swore that she would return after her death to haunt the house.

Nicholas, filled with a mixture of remorse and fear, decided to have the carpet folded into a wooden box and the lid nailed down. He then had it hidden in an attic out of temptation's way. He died in 1788 and remained true to his promise to Dame Armine. Some eighty years later the then Mrs le Strange, a beautiful American lady, discovered the carpet and, somewhat disappointed by its condition, decided to cut it up and distribute it as hearthrugs among the less forunate families in the nearby village.

She set out one morning on her mission of charity and after a rewarding day's work she returned in high spirits to the hall as evening drew in. As her carriage approached the magnificent gatehouse she suddenly caught sight of the unfamiliar face of a dishevelled, distraught and angry old woman glaring at her from one of the windows of the house. That evening she recognized the face of the woman as Dame Armine, from a family portrait in the house, and consulted her husband who quickly remembered the story of her deathbed threat. Mrs le Strange considered it to be fanciful at first but as the hauntings became more frequent she was forced to retrace the rugs and sew the carpet back together again.

But Dame Armine's ghost is still said to haunt the house and as it is now divided up into separate flats after a serious fire in 1953 perhaps this is what now angers the old lady?

NANTEOS HOUSE

Cardiganshire, Wales

So pass I hostel, hall and grange;
By bridge and fore, by park and pale,
All-arm'd I ride, whate'er betide,
Until I find the Holy Grail.

Sir Galahad,
Alfred Lord Tennyson (1809–1892)

KNOWN as the 'Treasure House of Wales' Nanteos once contained many fine paintings and ornaments. Among its visitors it numbers the poet Swinburne and the composer Wagner, who wrote part of his opera *Parsifal* here. But the greatest treasure of all at Nanteos, and perhaps the most precious object in the whole world, was the Holy Grail, the cup that was used at the Last Supper.

This wooden cup is believed to have miraculous healing powers. It is thought to have been brought to Glastonbury by Joseph of Arimathea. During the Dissolution of the monasteries under Henry VIII it was taken to Strata Florida Abbey, about twenty miles from Nanteos, in Wales. When Henry's men began to close in on the abbey it was smuggled over the hills to Nanteos and entrusted to the monks who were hiding there.

The dying words of the last monk at Nanteos were that the resident family should protect the cup 'until the church shall claim her own'. The resident Powell family obeyed these wishes until 1952 when their line died out and a major and Mrs Merrilees bought the house. It was sold again in 1967 and although they left the works of art the cup was said to have been taken to their new home in Herefordshire and deposited in a bank where it remains to this day.

Mrs Colegate, the present owner, is a larger than life character who is dedicated to the upkeep of the house against all odds. She has filled many of the dilapidated rooms with antiques and unusual tableaux, and also told me that Nanteos was 'alive with ghosts'.

One apparition is that of a huntsman, who broke his neck in a fall on the driveway while his wife was staring anxiously out of the window, waiting for his return. She later had the window blocked up so that she would never see this view

THE MUSIC ROOM

'TABLEAU', NANTEOS HOUSE

again. Another spirit is that of a man called Griffiths-Evans, who played the harp every Christmas for sixty-three years at the house; he died aged ninety. His ghost has been seen in the music room, with its Italian marble fireplace and exquisite plasterwork.

There is also the ghost known as the 'Jewel Lady' who in real life left her deathbed to hide her jewel box and her spirit appears to be vainly searching for it. Mrs Colegate says that people have even dredged the lake to find the jewels.

In the dark and dank cellars there is the spectre of a monk — the locals say that monks were buried there — and my wife in fact refused to descend the stairs as she felt so uneasy. Mrs Colegate showed me a newspaper cutting from the *Western Mail* dated 19 June 1984 telling how a TV crew came to make a film at Nanteos but after only two days the

cast and crew refused to work after dark. They said that the ghost of a man in a cloak appeared during filming, a broken music box would suddenly start to play, doors opened and closed without warning and props were mysteriously moved.

While I was talking to Mrs Colegate a former tenant of the house came in and told me how a friend of hers had been prevented from walking up the drive to the house by what she described as 'a line of force'. She had to telephone from the nearest town to be collected by car some hours later.

By now my wife and I were ready to leave although Mrs Colegate assured us that she lived quite happily along-side these apparitions. However, we felt that the longer we stayed the harder it would become for us to differentiate between the tableaux, the ghosts, and what we as mere mortals, presume to be reality.

DUNWICH

Suffolk, England

DUNWICH, at one time the ancient capital of East Anglia, boasted 52 churches, a bishop's palace, a mayor's mansion and ancient bronze gates of an immense size. Now just a few houses for the remaining fishermen, a church, and the eerie ruins of a priory and a leper hospital are all that remain after 700 years of coastal erosion. During a great storm in 1328 the city was engulfed by the sea and old Dunwich now lies beneath the ever advancing waves. Legend tells that the toll of phantom church bells can still be heard from their watery grave.

Latter-day Dunwich is unique in that the living mix openly with the dead, for along the clifftops skeletons can be seen protruding from their graves as the sea advances on the old graveyards. The poet Swinburne immortalized this in verse:

> Tombs, with bare white piteous bones protruded,
> Shroudless, down the loose collapsing banks,
> Crumble, from their constant place detruded,
> That the sea devours and gives not thanks.
> Graves where hope and prayer and sorrow brooded,
> Gape and slide and perish, ranks on ranks.
>
> *Dunwich*,
> Algernon Charles Swinburne (1837–1909)

It is said that strange shrouded figures have been seen wandering on the clifftops and they are believed to be ghosts of Dunwich's former citizens returned from the sea. On the day I visited I climbed up to the cliffs and came across the one remaining tombstone still standing facing the ocean. As I was getting out my camera I was joined by an elderly man who told me that he had lived near Dunwich all his life, and

GREYFRIARS PRIORY, DUNWICH

LAST REMAINING TOMBSTONE, CLIFFTOP, DUNWICH

that he could remember when the graveyard had been full of tombstones. Over the years he had watched it crumble and remembered how, when they were children, they would cycle along the cliffs and one day they played a practical joke on one of the girls by hiding a skull in her bicycle bag.

The old man then went on to tell me of the ghosts that

[98]

haunt Dunwich. He said that at night mysterious lights had been seen at the ruins of Greyfriars Priory and the chanting of the monks was often heard near the magnificent gateway to the abbey. Strange deformed figures have been seen in the graveyard near the Leper Hospital and the ghost of a demented young man wanders in the wooded pathways near the priory searching for his missing bride who left him for another man.

As I began to make my way back to my car along the beach I took one final look back towards the clifftops to see if the old man was still there, or could he too, perhaps, have returned to the sea?

WOODSTOCK HOUSE
County Kilkenny, Southern Ireland

THE home of the Tighe family, who were sympathetic to the Irish cause, Woodstock contained one of the finest libraries in Ireland and the demesne boasted rare shrubs and flora including the longest and most magnificent avenue of monkey puzzle trees in Europe. The house itself was built in 1740 and sadly burnt in 1922. Mary Tighe the poetess passed the latter part of her life here and it is her ghost that is said to haunt the grounds.

She was young, beautiful and gifted and this made her the centre of attention in Dublin society at that time. Born Mary Blackford she married her cousin, Henry Tighe, in October 1793 when she was twenty years old. Her famous poem 'Psyche or the Legend of Love' was published in 1795 but in 1805 she fell ill from consumption. One morning in 1810 she walked down from the house to the nearby village of Inistioge and on returning collapsed on a sofa and died. The famous sculptor Flaxman was duly summoned to make a cast of her reposing. He took three days to reach Woodstock but no one moved her. This monument to her can be found in a small neoclassical mausoleum in the Protestant churchyard at Inistioge.

A local told me that her ghost is most often seen retracing the steps of her last fateful walk, a pale and fragile figure, as graceful in death as she was in life.

I visited Woodstock at eight on a beautiful summer's evening. It is a majestic and peaceful place and the house itself, although long deserted, seemed to be strangely alive with ghostly figures.

MONUMENT TO MARY TIGHE, INISTIOGE CHURCHYARD

ETHIE CASTLE

Angus, Scotland

THE ancestral home of the Northesks for eleven centuries, this impressive castle near Arbroath is currently the home of Ann and Alistair Forsyth of that Ilk, heads of the Clan Forsyth.

During the sixteenth century the castle was the favourite resort of the infamous Cardinal Beaton, Abbot of Arbroath in 1524, who had several homes in the area, and the ghost of the murdered prelate is said to haunt its corridors.

The Catholic Cardinal was merciless to his opponents and unscrupulous in the pursuit of his aims. He is said to have taken delight in burning Protestants, while he himself indulged in a life-style quite unbefitting to a man of God, especially of such high rank. Beaton's reputation with women was notorious and he rented Ethie to his favourite mistress, Marion Ogilvie, who bore him several children. Eventually the Cardinal's sins overtook him and he was brutally assassinated by a band of Protestant noblemen at St Andrews Castle on 29 May 1546.

His ghost has been seen in the house but, more frequently, the weird thumping sound of his leg being dragged slowly up the original stone stairway to his bedchamber in the attic has been heard. Towards the end of his life he suffered from severe attacks of gout in one leg and it had to be bound in cloth. The bedroom is still known as the 'haunted chamber' and 'Old Fyvie', the housekeeper at Ethie for a lifetime,

CARDINAL BEATON (1494–1546)

DAVID BETONIVS S·R·E· CARD· ARCHIEP· S· ANDREÆ
IN SCOTIA AB HOSTIBVS FIDEI BARBARE TRVCIDATVS

would tell how she used to barricade her door at night against this terrible sound.

There are other gruesome stories attached to the castle. One tells of a governess who came to stay in an old part of the castle that had been shut up for a long time. For several nights she was woken by a child's sobs, footsteps above her head, and the sound of a toy being wheeled across the

ceiling. The entrance to the room above her had been bricked up but following these uncanny noises it was broken into and the skeleton of a child and the remnants of a wooden cart were discovered. After they had been given a Christian burial the noises ceased.

Another ghost is that of the 'Green Lady' who appeared when a member of the Northesk family was about to die.

The most recent occurrence was when the Earl of Northesk died in London and she appeared to several members of the family in the 'tapestry room'.

Ann Forsyth, an intelligent and intriguing woman, eagerly showed me the Cardinal's chapel and the 'haunted chamber' saying that she felt his presence in the old part of the house but did not feel at all alarmed by it.

[103]

WINTER'S GIBBET
Northumberland, England

A FEW miles from Elsdon, high up on the wild and windswept Northumbrian moors, stands Winter's Gibbet, so named because a man called William Winter was hung in chains there in 1791 for murdering a lonely old lady called Margaret Crozier. It was said to be the last time the gibbet was used in England.

Margaret Crozier lived at Raw Pele, an ancient tower two miles north of Elsdon, situated on a pedlar's way much used by travellers and gypsies. She kept a small drapery shop in the tower and also, rumour had it, a secret hoard of money. It was there that she was found one day with her throat cut. Suspicion immediately fell on Winter, a man with a fearsome reputation, and two female companions, all gypsies, who had been seen in the district during the previous week.

Winter admitted the robbery but the three denied murdering her. They were eventually convicted on the damning evidence of a local shepherd boy, and were hanged in Newcastle. The bodies of the women were given to the Surgeons Hall for dissection, but for Winter a worse fate lay in store. His body was to be hung in chains and left to rot until the bones were picked clean by crows.

A prominent place overlooking the scene of the crime was chosen for the gibbet, which stands there to this day. A wooden effigy of his head remains as a macabre attraction for passers by. It is said that, late at night, the creaking of his skeleton can still be heard in the wind as one passes by the gibbet and at nearby Raw Pele shadowy figures are sometimes seen fleeing from the tower.

THE PEDIMENTED ARCH

ARCH HALL

County Meath, Southern Ireland

THE HOUSE has the unlikely appearance of a French château and derives its name from a pedimented arch in the grounds. The present sensitive owner of the Hall, Mrs Kitty Colwell, lives in the nearby farmhouse and was very forthcoming on the history of Arch Hall. Before she moved into the farm people had told her to beware as the hall and land were both badly haunted and at first she was terrified by their stories of ghostly hands and other phantom visitors. On one of her first nights there, when she went out to check on the animals in the stables, she saw a badger — and thought it was the Devil.

Mrs Colwell told me that the previous owner of the Hall, a Mrs Gillette, had lived there with two different husbands and was a very imposing figure who had suffered greatly during her life-time. She had originally been in love with Mr Gillette but first was forced to marry a Mr Garnett whom she did not care for but in the end she captured her true love. She had two sons and a daughter from her first marriage. One son died in World War I and the other returned from the fighting somewhat deranged. According to Mrs Colwell he would shoot at anything in sight and then order the servants to nail it to the walls of the house and leave it to rot. The daughter Connie was very much younger, very beautiful and a very good horsewoman.

One room in the Hall, Mrs Colwell told me, was completely in gold, from the paint, to the furniture, to the picture frames, but this was all destroyed or stolen by the IRA when they burnt the house in 1922.

The ghosts in the Hall were many and a strange story is told by a young woman who was staying there for a house party during the Garnetts' time. It appears she saw a strange man and woman come down the main stairs arm in arm in evening dress on the night of the ball. Later she said to Mrs Garnett 'You didn't tell me that you had other guests staying in the house', who replied, 'We haven't, they are just our friends from the past.' The young lady left the same evening.

[105]

ABBOTSFORD HOUSE
Roxburghshire, Scotland

BUILT by the romantic novelist Sir Walter Scott between 1817 and 1825, this large turreted house was his 'dream'. Sir Walter was interested in all forms of the occult and experienced several supernatural encounters himself, one of these occurring within the first year of the house's construction.

One night he heard noises that sounded like the violent dragging of heavy boards along the new part of the house.

INTERIORS, ABBOTSFORD HOUSE

SIR WALTER SCOTT (1771–1832)

Carrying out a lengthy investigation, whilst armed with a broadsword, he was unable to discover anything. It was uncanny, however, to discover next day that his agent, George Bullock, who had designed that part of the house, had suddenly died at the time the noises were at their height. They were never heard again.

Shortly after the house was completed financial ruin overtook Scott and creditors seized the house. By the time he was able to regain control he was already close to death. His ghost has been seen many times gazing out of the dining-room window. He had requested that his bed be placed there during his final hours, so that he could take one last look at his beloved countryside.

The house still contains a very fine collection of armour and relics of various Scottish heroes, and one has the uneasy feeling that the ghosts of history are closely following one's every step through the corridors of the mansion.

WARKWORTH CASTLE

Northumberland, England

THE castle, which stands on the summit of a precipitous hill, was originally built in the twelfth century as a fortification against the marauding Scots, and passed into the hands of the powerful Percy family in the fourteenth century. About half a mile from the castle, hidden on a heavily wooded river bank, are the remains of a hermitage, hewn in the rock. It can still be reached by ferry boat and consists of a chapel and living quarters. It is a beautiful and lonely place, but conceals the tragic and harrowing tale of the ghost that haunts this estate.

Legend tells how Bertram de Bothal of Bothal Castle, owing allegiance to the then Lord Percy, fell in love with the beautiful Lady Isabel Widdrington. Although she greatly desired the young man, she wished to see further proof of his love for her. She presented him with an engraved helmet, commanding him to wear it bravely in battle to win her honour and hand in marriage.

Not long afterwards Bertram was presented with his chance. Lord Percy, or Harry 'Hotspur' as he was known for his exceptional feats of bravery, crossed the border with some of his men in pursuit of Scottish raiders. In the battle that ensued, Bertram fought with great courage but was seriously injured and had to be taken back to England for his wounds to heal. Isabel's father was told of Bertram's bravery and Isabel, feeling guilty about her foolish challenge, hastened to nurse him. Unknown to her father she set out with only a single manservant to guard her. A week went by but Isabel did not arrive. Bertram, not yet fully recovered but fearing the worst, left his bed and set out with his younger brother to search the Borderlands for her. They crossed into Scotland and decided to go different ways in order to cover a wider area.

Several days later Bertram learnt that Isabel was held prisoner in the castle of a notorious Border raider. He hastened to the castle where he kept watch from a nearby cave. By now he was growing very weak from his wounds and could not see how he would be able to climb the castle's steep walls to rescue her. On the second night he was awakened from his sleep by the sound of voices. He saw the figure of a woman climbing down a rope from the tower and a man dressed in tartan holding the end of the rope.

Bertram immediately recognized the woman as Isabel and followed the couple until they were out of sight of the castle. He then advanced towards them, his sword drawn, demanding that the Scotsman give up his love. Beside himself with rage he struck out at his rival, who fell to the ground before he had time to reply. Bertram raised his sword to strike another blow but Isabel flung herself between them and in doing so received the full force of his sword, falling mortally wounded. With her dying words she explained how his brother, disguised as a Scots raider, had discovered where she was being held and had arranged for her escape. It was his own brother that he had killed.

Beside himself with grief Bertram returned to Northumberland where Lord Percy granted him sanctuary at Warkworth Castle. Before long Bertram, racked by guilt, gave away all his wealth and possessions, leaving the castle to build the hermitage nearby. He carved the chapel out of the rock-face and here he spent many lonely hours in prayer and meditation until his eventual death. Carved into the rock of the chapel he left this pitiful message in Latin:

'My tears have been my meat, by day and by night.'

It is his inconsolable ghost that still haunts the hermitage and castle.

MINSTER LOVELL HALL
Oxfordshire, England

THE IMPOSING ruins of Minster Lovell Hall, home of the Lovell family, stand beside the River Windrush, near Thame. Disappearance and tragedy seem to have haunted the Lovell lineage since the fifteenth century. One of those to suffer was Francis, the first Viscount Lovell. He was devoted to his king, the 'infamous' Richard III, and by supporting him at the battle of Bosworth in 1485, he put his own life in jeopardy. After Richard's defeat and death in the battle, Francis was forced to flee to Minster Lovell. There he hid, locked in a secret chamber. His retainers had all deserted him except his old housekeeper. She knew the location of the room and willingly looked after him and fed him. However, she suddenly died and as there was nobody else who knew of his whereabouts, he was left to waste away and die. In 1708 some workmen who were restoring the mansion came across a secret panel. When they opened it they found a walled cell and inside, sitting at a table, was a human skeleton. The remains of a dog were lying at his feet. Within minutes of the discovery both skeletons crumbled into dust.

The most famous story attached to Minster Lovell has become known over the years as the 'Mistletoe Bough'. One Christmas the Hall was adorned with all the traditional seasonal decorations, but there was to be a very special celebration that night too, a party to honour the wedding of young William Lovell, the eldest son of the family, and his beautiful young bride.

The Lovells and their guests danced all evening and then, as midnight approached, someone suggested that they should play hide and seek. The young bride offered to hide, teasing her husband by imploring him to find her first. She ran off and the remainder of the company left a suitable interval before they began to search for her. But no one could find her and after a while young Lovell became distraught, crying out her name, pleading with her to reveal her hiding place. They looked for her all that night and all of the next day, but to no avail. For a week they searched the grounds, but they never found her. Young Lovell could not face life without her and as the years went by he became embittered and remorseful until he finally died of a broken heart.

Some time later one of the servants discovered an old oak chest that had been hidden in the attic. When he raised the lid, he recoiled in horror, for inside lay a mouldering skeleton dressed in a bridal gown. In her excitement the young girl had climbed into the chest to hide but as she lay there, keeping as still as possible, the lid had fallen, locking her in a living tomb. Even now, amid the ruins of the hall, the desperate cries of William Lovell are said to be heard as he continues his hopeless search.

THE ICKNIELD WAY

near Swyncombe Downs, Oxfordshire, England

A PREHISTORIC road winds across England from the Wash on the east coast into Wiltshire on the west and has been known from ancient times as the Icknield Way. The track is still easy to follow except where it has either become overgrown or sadly been destroyed. This ancient pathway is said to harbour many ghosts along its course including Roman Legionaries, phantom coaches and black dogs. There are also those who claim to have witnessed the apparitions of Queen Boadicea's charioteers who careered along it on their way to sack St Albans in AD 61.

I photographed a part of the Way that passes by Swyncombe Downs near Watlington in Oxfordshire and which has been believed over many centuries to lead to the World's End and from there into the depths of hell. This is a truly mysterious site.

RUSHTON TRIANGULAR LODGE

Northamptonshire, England

THOMAS TRESHAM of Rushton Hall was born a Protestant, and inherited his father's vast wealth and estates in 1560 at the age of fifteen. He was knighted by Elizabeth I in 1576 but, shortly after, he made the then momentous decision to renounce the Protestant church and take on the illegal Catholic faith. For this act of conscience he was to spend the next fifteen years of his life, on and off, in prison and it was there that he conceived the plans for his extraordinary building, the Triangular Lodge. When finally released he began to build the Lodge, a symbol of the Holy Trinity in that everything in or on the building was divisible by the number three. The grounds were even laid out in a triangle containing nine trees and the building took three years to complete.

On his death in 1605 his eldest son Francis inherited the estate but was implicated in the Gunpowder Plot and died in the Tower the same year. It is believed that the conspirators may have met in the Lodge on several occasions. After Francis's death it was boarded up and fell into ruin.

The ghost of a gypsy is said to haunt the Lodge. In the eighteenth century the estate was owned by Lord Robert Cullen who discovered a secret underground passage thought to lead from the Lodge to the Hall. The tunnel appeared dangerous and Lord Cullen offered fifty pounds to any man who would dare to explore it. The offer was taken up by a gypsy fiddler who entered the passage with a lantern tied around his waist. His fiddle was heard for a time but then suddenly stopped, the tunnel collapsed, and he was never seen again. It was bricked up with the gypsy inside and it is said that his fiddle can still sometimes be heard.

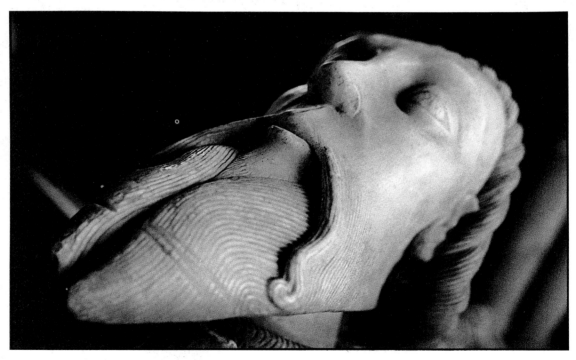

ALABASTER MONUMENT TO SIR THOMAS TRESHAM,
RUSHTON CHURCH

DACRE CASTLE
Cumberland, England

THIS fourteenth-century stronghold of the powerful Dacre family was once the meeting place of three kings in ancient times in an unsuccessful attempt to sign a peace treaty between England and Scotland. Their remorseful ghosts are still said to be seen at the castle to this day.

A more detailed and ghastly haunting is recorded by Rebecca Dane and Craig MacNeale in their book *Strange and Supernatural*. It began in the fifteenth century, when a young heir to the castle, Sir Guy Dacre, fell in love with the daughter of a French nobleman who was a friend of his father. Her name was Eloise. Unfortunately for Guy she spurned his advances and so he asked his Italian tutor, a handsome man, to help him win her heart. But while Guy was away fighting in Scotland the two became lovers, although Guy remained unaware of their affair. On his return Eloise married Guy, who still suspected nothing.

Soon Guy was forced to leave again for Scotland and he entrusted the castle to his loyal friend Lyulph. His friend was suspicious of the two lovers and became incensed by the fool they were making of Guy. Eventually the lovers left to live in York together and the friend felt obliged to tell Guy. On hearing the tragic news Guy rode straight back to York but the Italian had fled, not knowing that Lyulph was waiting for him. Guy captured Eloise and took her, securely bound, back to Dacre. He led her down a dark passage to a dungeon that she had never seen before, untied her, and locked her in. There she saw her lover chained to a wall. She rushed towards him to kiss him but, as her hand caressed his face, his head rolled from his shoulders to the floor.

She was kept locked in the cell until she gradually went insane and finally died beside the rotting corpse of her lover. Their pathetic ghosts, not surprisingly, haunt the castle.

CADEBY HALL

Lincolnshire, England

CADEBY HALL lies in a secluded valley between
the old Roman road of Barton Street and the foot of
the Lincolnshire Wolds near the market town of
Louth. The parkland contains a variety of tall, old trees
and lying among them is a prehistoric mound.

Cadeby's history is difficult to trace but there appears
to have been a house there since 1700. It would seem to
have been built on the site of a monastery as the remains
of a small reservoir, known to the locals as the 'Monks
Bath', and a chapel and underground passages can still
be seen. The house has always been reputed to have been
'haunted' and is in fact cursed. It appears that a small boy
of just seven years old went missing one day in the
grounds and despite an extensive search he was not found.

AN ENTRANCE TO THE CELLARS, CADEBY HALL

Years later some workmen discovered his skeleton in the hollow of a tree. His distraught mother put a curse on Cadeby to the effect that the eldest son of whoever owned and lived in Cadeby Hall would not inherit the house.

Before this curse ghost stories abounded at the hall. A ghostly coach and four horses would drive up to the house on a night when a member of the owner's family died. People also reported seeing a hooded monk follow them along the 'Monks Walk' in the garden, which would then fade away. The servants complained of hearing clanking chains in the underground passages, and of doors that even when securely locked at night would be found wide open in the morning. Several heavy chains were found suspended in the tunnels and having been removed the passages were eventually blocked up. One was said to lead to the nunnery at nearby North Ormsby, and another to Wyham House.

At present the hall is rented by the Abbots, who live nearby. Mr Abbot told me that he knew of the house's evil reputation and preferred to live elsewhere. The house has remained empty for some time.

As we were leaving Cadeby by Barton Street my brother pointed out a stone memorial at the roadside almost opposite Cadeby's driveway, dedicated to sixteen-year-old George Nelson of Cadeby Hall, who was killed when his horse shied at lightning during a storm on 16 January, 1885. He then showed me the following letter in a recent copy of the local newspaper:

Sir, a friend of mine was driving a lorry during the early hours of the morning last November along Barton Street near Cadeby Hall when a man on horseback came out in front of him. The horse reared up and threw the rider into the dyke. He stopped to see if the rider was injured but there was no one there. Is there any record of anyone else seeing this horse or rider?

CURRY MALLET MANOR

Somerset, England

MRS Deta Mallet can prove direct descent from a Norman knight who fought at the Battle of Hastings in 1066. In fact the Mallet coat-of-arms is included in the Bayeux tapestry. Mallet Manor was once a strong Saxon castle but was converted in the seventeenth century in typical Tudor fashion. Three different kings are said to have dined in the house's banqueting hall: William the Conqueror, Henry II and King John. The Mallet's historical deeds are too numerous to mention here but many ghosts still haunt the house and grounds.

A lady in Elizabethan clothes is said to wander the corridors, carrying her keys at her waistband, and she is very house-proud. On a certain night of the year two men can be heard duelling in the courtyard, outside what used to be the keep of the old castle. The figure of a dapper, slim man can sometimes be seen pacing up and down the Great Hall dressed in Elizabethan clothes. There is also a letter in existence, from this man it is presumed, saying he had heard that the Armada was coming up the Channel and it states, 'I spent last night walking up and down the house praying for England.'

Mrs Mallet is deeply attached to the house and gardens and as we walked outside she told me of a gentleman who had visited some years before who claimed to have psychic powers, and who had told her that the house had many ghosts — but the gardens were 'teeming' with them.

According to Mrs Mallet, from the times when the house had been a castle there had been a tilting or jousting arena where tournaments were held and this was now covered by the gardens. She also told me that several skeletons had at various times been dug up in the gardens. All these stories were recounted in a calm and dignified voice as if they were quite normal occurrences and it left me with an uneasy feeling that I was part of a 'ghostly tapestry' that at any moment might come alive.

MRS DETA MALLET AND DAUGHTER

'Haunted Garden', Curry Mallet Manor

PLAS PREN
Denbighshire, Wales

WHILE driving over the desolate moors of North Wales one summer's evening my wife suddenly exclaimed, 'Look at that house. It's perfect for your book'. She was pointing to a mysterious and spectacular ruin lying high up on a hill about a mile ahead of us. With a feeling of great anticipation we drove towards it, noticing that it stood on its own, the only building for miles around being a public house on the road near its overgrown driveway.

We left the car by the Sportsman's Arms, and slowly strolled up the drive. We passed a few old gnarled trees and ahead of us we could see several sheep circling the house, sometimes stopping to stare at us as we approached. The house close up was just as awe-inspiring as from a distance and had a strangely 'oppressive' feel, as if something quite terrible had once happened there. As the sun was beginning to set and we both had a thirst we decided to return to the pub and see if we could discover some of the house's history.

In the bar we met some of the locals who told us that Plas Pren had been built by a Lord Davenport as a shooting lodge in the early part of this century. The area was well known for its excellent grouse shooting but due to the house's isolation and the difficulty in obtaining servants it had been sold in 1925. For the next twenty-five years it was lived in by the estate gamekeepers, and was eventually abandoned in the 1950s, remaining derelict ever since. When I asked why this had happened there was a silence, but one man told me that he had once heard a strange story about the house.

Apparently several years ago two young lovers had visited the ruin late at night and had claimed to have seen 'something' unearthly. When questioned further they described it as a tall 'luminous' skeleton that glowed in the dark as it approached them. Needless to say they ran for their lives.

KNEBWORTH HOUSE
Hertfordshire, England

KNEBWORTH House is the ancestral home of the Lytton family, of whom Edward Bulwer-Lytton is remembered for his interest in occult studies as well as his numerous political achievements. He was a leading member of the Rosicrucian Society in England and this influenced his writings in the genre. Amongst the better known of these works are the novel *Zanoni* and the chilling short story 'The Haunters And The Haunted' or 'The House And The Brain'.

Having passed up the long driveway we were met at the front door by the wife of the present owner, Lady Lytton Cobbold, who invited us inside for tea. She expressed her own interest in ghosts and told us some of her experiences as a little girl at her former home, Hartland Abbey, in Devon.

After tea she produced some ancient handwritten manuscripts relating to some of Knebworth's own ghostly inhabitants, the most famous of these being the sad 'Jenny Spinner' who, for committing some dreadful crime, was imprisoned in the east wing of the house with only her spinning wheel for company. She eventually went mad and died. At frequent intervals after her death the sound of her spinning wheel could be heard late at night.

EDWARD BULWER-LYTTON (1803–1873)

BULWER-LYTTON'S STUDY, KNEBWORTH HOUSE

Another document tells of the haunted Beauchamp Chamber where a visitor to the house in 1724 encountered the ghost of a beautiful but dreadfully distressed young woman during the night. She revealed to him a secret panel in the bedroom wall. When opened the next day the hiding place contained a vial of poison and a lock of hair, certain clues to the unfortunate girl's guilt or own sad demise.

Lady Lytton-Cobbold also spoke of the ghost of a man which several members of the family have seen in the picture gallery of the house, but who this was she did not know.

Before we left we walked once more around the house, inspired by the Gothic architecture and the strange Indian landscaped gardens, and could not help wondering what it was that had so affected Bulwer-Lytton during his lifetime for him to have created such an extraordinary fantasy world to live in.

KNEBWORTH HOUSE

ACKNOWLEDGMENTS

Thank you to the following for their help, inspiration and support over the years: My family, Ruth Barclay, Stephanie Bennett, Jody and Muffy Burns, Nick Morris, Sheridan Coakley, Nigel Coke, David Larcher, John Meaker, Richard Adams, Pete Turner, Carol Janeway, Peter Glidewell, Duncan McLaren, Keith Collie, Dana Johnson, Ruan and Jackie O'Lochlainn, Anthony and Martine Moore, Sam Wagstaffe, Gilly Goschen, Napier and Tricia Russell, Karen Russo, Adrian Knowles, Russ Anderson and Maggie Weston, Peter Blegvad, Claudia Boulton, Lod Sharpe, Claudine Maugendre, Alan Chasanoff, Piers and Miriam Rogers, John May, Peter Ryan, Françoise and Isabelle Vasseur, Calvin Fentress, Dirk Zimmer, Kathy John, Jerry Miller, Michael Palin, Peggy Kessler and Ladd Yunque, Peter Reid, Nick and Cheryl Fairrie, Mark Edwards, Chris Steele-Perkins, Tricia Bell, Mr Wesencraft (The Harry Price Library), Shyamoli Sen, Melvyn Harris, Joshua Friewald, Paul Stratherne, Delian Bower, Vic Giolitto and Colin Wilson.

A special thank you to Caroline Carey for her encouragement, patience and invaluable research work, and to my wife, Cassie, who helped and motivated me to finish the book.

Final appreciation to all those landlords, librarians and owners of haunted houses the length and breadth of the British Isles and Ireland for their kindness, help and hospitality.

SELF-PORTRAIT

PICTURE CREDITS

The author and publishers would like to thank the following for supplying illustrations:

The British Museum   88
Earl of Lonsdale   14
A private Scottish collection   102

Museo Lazaro, Madrid   50
National Portrait Gallery   24, 34, 73 (below), 108 (below)
Scottish National Portrait Gallery   28
University of London (Mary Evans Picture Library/Harry Price Library)   37 (above), 40, 56, 69, 70, 90, 125 (above)

DATE DUE
